HOME CHANGES
THE LONG ROAD HOME
BOOK TWENTY-TWO

KRIS MICHAELS

Copyright © 2025 by Kris Michaels

All rights reserved.

No part of this book may be reproduced in any form or by any electronic or mechanical means, including information storage and retrieval systems, without written permission from the author, except for the use of brief quotations in a book review.

CHAPTER 1

Seth Hansen adjusted the leash at his side as he approached the Airline Special Services counter near the North Terminal at Hartsfield-Jackson. Gomer's retirement orders were freshly printed and crisp in the folder tucked beneath his arm, and the large black German Shepherd sitting obediently at his heel drew quiet stares from travelers.

"Ma'am," he said when the people in front of him moved away from the counter, handing over the travel orders and information for his partner. "I'm the handler for MWD Gomer. He's PCS-ing to his retirement in South Dakota."

Gomer had been a military working dog for years in the Air Force, and Seth had been the kennel master when Gomer came on duty. That, of course, was before Seth had been promoted and started shuffling paperwork for his major command. The higher his rank, the farther he moved from the MWDs. But he kept his ear to the ground and his eyes open. Six months after he'd retired, he'd discovered Gomer was being retired due to arthritis in his hips. Seth had jumped at the chance to adopt Gomer and give him a forever home. He'd known exactly who to contact, and within a month, Gomer had officially been his. As a final thank you for Seth and Gomer's service, the MWD was given retirement orders to cover the cost of his transportation to South Dakota. Not that Seth cared. He would've paid any price to have this special dog at his side.

The agent, a middle-aged woman with weary eyes and a practiced smile, took the documents and began typing.

Seth handed her the folder. "I've got his medical clearance, crate specs, and transfer authorization," Seth added, giving Gomer a reassuring pat behind the ear. The crate was on a trolley behind them.

The woman was efficient and motioned for the skycap to bring the large crate over. Seth slipped the guy a ten-spot and turned back to the woman, who printed and applied cargo labels to the crate.

Turning back to him, she lifted a finger. "Give me a minute, sir." She tapped on the computer and shook her head. "I hate to be the one to say it, but all outbound flights to the Midwest are on hold because a massive weather system over Denver has caused cascading delays." She tapped a few more keys and looked up. "It'll be hours. Realistically, it could be six or more." She almost winced when she told him. "I'm sorry."

He cocked his head. "You can't control the weather." He glanced down at Gomer. "I'm not going to put him in a crate until I have to."

"I understand," the woman said. "It wouldn't be kind." She handed him a map and circled an area. "Here's the best area where you can go outside quickly and let him relieve himself. We've worked through our fair share of delays and learned that most handlers won't release their dogs until the last minute." She smiled at him. "Unlike some others. I've seen all kinds." She shrugged.

Seth nodded and clenched his jaw. He'd also seen his share of people who shouldn't own an animal. He tightened the leash, but the dog didn't react, just sat like a stone, waiting for his next command. "Roger that, I know exactly what you mean," Seth said quietly, calculating his next move. He blinked and snapped his gaze back to her. "Is the USO still open?"

The woman looked at her watch. "It is. Do you know where it is?"

"I do. Been through here many times. Thank you, and we'll be back as soon as we have a firm departure time."

"If you give me your number, I'll text you when we get the clearance to start loading. That would give you enough time to get through security before you board, but you'd have to hustle to your gate."

"I'm not adverse to a jog through the airport." Seth smiled at her as he told her his number.

She wrote it down on Gomer's documents. "If the delay lasts past my shift, I'll ensure my relief understands to contact you."

"Thank you." He looked down at Gomer. "Heel." The animal moved instantly, walking at Seth's heel with no room between the dog's shoulder and his leg. He waited for people to clear the escalator before lifting Gomer and stepping onto the moving metal. Gomer was a solid eighty-five pounds, and none of it was fat. He was a King Shepherd, tall and almost lanky. When Seth stepped off the escalator, he carried the dog away from the exit before putting him down safely. Gomer's tongue lashed him with a wet kiss as soon as his feet hit the ground.

Laughing, Seth wiped off the affection. "You're such a goober." He ruffled Gomer's scruff and let the dog relax for a moment. After a brief pause, Seth waited for a break in the flow of people before he and Gomer headed toward the USO. Maybe he could find a quiet corner for Gomer to relax and chill. Lord knew he needed the downtime before returning to South Dakota. His father's decline was more than enough for Seth to put his plans on hold and move back home to ensure the old man didn't get into more trouble.

He'd only been there a week when he'd gotten the call to pick up Gomer. Ken, the sheriff in the county, and his deputies were taking turns checking in on Chester, making sure he didn't cause any trouble. The man was cantankerous even on his best days. On a bad day, well, he was pure hell to be around. But Chester had worked hard all his life, giving Seth and his sister Sarah a strong ethical upbringing, even though his old man had never hugged them, told them he loved them, or said it to their mom. God rest her soul. She was a saint. Seth would never be a saint, but he'd be a good son and figure out how to get his dad the help he needed. Hopefully.

He approached the USO sign-in desk, and the woman behind it smiled widely. Her dark hair and brilliant smile made her seem ageless, but he'd peg her in her late forties. Maybe. It was hard to tell.

"Welcome." She stepped out and leaned down. "Hi, Gomer, how have you been, boy?"

Seth frowned, absolutely confused. "How did you …"

The woman flicked her hand at him, dismissing his question. "Oh, Gomer was through here last year. He and his handler were coming back from a deployment. Weren't you, big boy?"

Gomer's tail swished, but the dog didn't move, although Seth could tell he wanted to. "Yes you were." She smiled widely.

He watched as the woman held out her hand, and Gomer dropped his head into it. She stroked his head with the other, saying, "I told you, didn't I? You got a forever home." She leaned forward and kissed Gomer's nose.

"What?" Seth asked her.

"Oh, nothing, just a conversation Gomer and I had last year." The woman stood up. "Heading to South Dakota?"

Seth blinked, and his mouth opened and then closed. "Ah, yeah, how did you know?"

The woman nodded to his shirt pocket. "Ticket."

He glanced down and looked at the paper ticket the agent at the Special Services Counter had given him to claim Gomer at the end of their flight. "Oh."

"Sign in, and we'll get you set up in the library. It's quiet there, and you and Gomer can relax without families and kids wanting to pet him. Even though I'm not worried about him, some kids can get grabby."

"Thanks, that would be appreciated. He's obedient but hasn't been exposed to many children, and the old guy might get cranky." Seth reached down and ruffled his scruff again. Gomer looked up, his tongue lolling to the side, and Seth laughed. "Such a goober."

The woman laughed. "The best goober. You know I have a very good friend. Her name is Kate Wells. She's a vet in a small town called Hollister. She used to work with MWDs as an Army vet. Her husband, Tegan, is a rancher up there."

"Hollister?" Seth's voice hit a register he didn't know he could hit. Gomer was immediately on alert.

She cocked her head. "You know Hollister?"

"I'm going there. I grew up there. I know Tegan. He was a couple of years younger than me. If I recall right, he was a quiet guy."

"That sounds like him." The woman extended her hand. "My name is Blessing." Seth took her hand and shook it. "Let's get you back and settled." She looked around. "You don't have a bag?"

"Just my backpack. I flew in yesterday, and I'm flying out today." His small pack held Gomer's papers, a change of clothes, a toothbrush, toothpaste, and deodorant, plus a bag of treats for Gomer. Traveling light was a thing.

"No laptop or business equipment?" Blessing asked as she walked him inside.

"Nope. Just retired and have some family obligations to pigeonhole before I start working again."

Blessing stopped and looked at him. "You want to pigeonhole your dad?"

"What? How did you know I was talking about my dad?"

"It was either that or your mom, and I didn't think anyone would say that about their mom." Blessing cocked her head. "You know, his being so grumpy might not be his fault. You should get him checked out medically."

"What?" It was the only word he seemed to know at the moment. Seth stopped and stared at the woman, who gave him a brilliant smile. "A good physical never hurt anyone, has it?" She turned and walked away. Seth stared at her until she looked over her shoulder and said, "Are you coming?"

"Yeah." He cleared his throat, and he and Gomer followed her into the back, where a vacant room had a couch and two chairs. He took the chair in the corner, instructed Gomer to lie down beside it, and took off his backpack. "This is fantastic. Thank you."

"No problem. I'll bring four more travelers back here, but they'll all be military or recently separated and won't cause a problem for you or Gomer." She turned to walk away but stopped and looked back at him. "I'm glad you're going home with him. You both need a permanent place to live."

Seth frowned and started to respond that Hollister wasn't his permanent home and never would be, but she'd walked out of the room. He glanced down at Gomer. "Did you get the woo-woo vibe?" Gomer rolled over on his side and groaned. Seth nodded. "Yeah, me, too."

After wrapping the leash around his leg, he leaned back in the chair and stroked Gomer's fur, letting the act soothe away the worry that had been constant since he'd seen his father. Alzheimer's was a bitch of a disease. His father's short-term memory was crap, and he was even more gruff and argumentative than the deputy who'd called his sister had led them to believe.

About thirty minutes later, Blessing was back. "Seth, this is Tyler Marconi, recently retired from the Army. He'll be on a flight north to Montana."

"If it ever leaves," Tyler said as he extended his hand toward Seth, putting Gomer immediately on alert.

"It's okay, bud," Seth said reassuringly to his dog as he took Tyler's hand and shook it.

"He's wearing an MWD harness," Tyler said, pointing out the obvious.

Seth chuckled. "Yep. He's going to South Dakota with me. He's retired, too."

Tyler smiled briefly and glanced at his phone.

"I'll let you two settle and be back shortly," Blessing said before leaving with a smile.

"Montana home for you?" Seth asked as Tyler sat down on the couch. Gomer sat up and stared at Tyler.

"Yeah. Is it okay to pet him?" He nodded toward Gomer.

"Sure. His name is Gomer," Seth said, watching the interaction between the two of them. Tyler extended his hand for Gomer to smell, which he did.

Then Tyler stroked his head, and Gomer's mouth opened, his tongue lolling out.

Tyler smiled. "He's beautiful."

"And getting up there in age. He has some hip issues, but we'll get him on some preventive supplements and maybe some meds to keep him healthy and comfortable." He was going to look up Tegan's wife as soon as he could.

Tyler glanced at his phone and dropped it on his lap, still petting Gomer.

"Everything okay?" Seth asked.

Tyler glanced at him and then focused on Gomer, petting him as he spoke. "My gramps ... the last of my family ... he's in the hospital, and they say he doesn't have long. I was in the middle of out-processing from Fort Moore when I got the call."

"Shit, dude, I'm sorry. They'll get the flights going soon. If we're on the same flight, I'll make sure you get a seat even if I have to give up mine." He wouldn't be able to pull Gomer out of his checked status, but there were a few things he'd make that sacrifice for, and one of them was saying goodbye to your family. It was why he was returning to Hollister to help with his dad. Family was important, even if it was dysfunctional.

"She said I'd make it." Tyler looked at him for a

split second before adding, "Blessing. I didn't say anything to her, but she seemed to know and said I'd make it in time."

Seth nodded. "She seems to know a lot that no one tells her. Trust that feeling in your gut. I plan on it." He would take his dad for a checkup, even if he had to hogtie him and tumble him in the bed of his truck to get him there.

Tyler's phone rang, and the man jumped up like his ass was on fire, then walked out while answering the phone. Seth reached down and stroked Gomer. "It's okay, bud. He's just worried. I know that feeling."

He watched Tyler pacing back and forth as he talked on the phone before finally disconnecting and heading back into the room.

"Everything okay?"

Tyler nodded and sat back down. "Still good. I have some time. Not much, but some." His hand went to Gomer's back, and he started petting the dog again. Seth watched as Gomer moved a bit closer and looked up at Tyler. The dog sensed the man's worry better than Seth ever could. Gomer was exactly what the man needed. Seth had been there and done that. When his mom had taken ill and he was deployed, his dog at the time, Bronx, was the thing that had kept him sane. Dogs knew shit humans would never understand.

Seth wished like hell he had some magic words to say to help the guy out. But dealing with death and older parents sucked more than just about anything. He was finding that out with a crash course in dementia and Alzheimer's. He'd read just about every article he could. Some new medicines delayed the process, but it was a slow and deadly killer. He hated that for his old man. Chester had never needed anything from anyone. He was fiercely independent, and that was a point of pride for his father.

Blessing walked in with her arm linked through that of another man. "Seth and Tyler, this is Codwell Drakos, he goes by Code. He's a retired Army Colonel."

Code made a face. "Lieutenant Colonel, and that's just a rank, not who I am." He reached out a hand to both Seth and Tyler.

Seth shook his hand, and Gomer sneezed, drawing attention to where he was lying between the chair and the couch.

Code looked at Gomer and asked, "What do we have here?"

Tyler chuckled and replied, "A dog, sir." Seth

couldn't help the laugh that fell from him at Tyler's comeback.

Code belted out a laugh, too. "Okay, I deserved that."

Blessing patted Code on the arm. "I'll be back shortly. I have two more for this room. They're running a bit late."

Code sat down and asked, "Where are you two heading?"

Seth and Tyler replied, and they visited for about a half an hour before Blessing came back into the room with the last two men. "Gentlemen, may I introduce Dean Sinclair and Noah Ziegler?" She turned to the newcomers and introduced the others. "This is Tyler Marconi, retired Army, heading to Montana. Seth Hansen, who's heading to South Dakota with his newly adopted and retired MWD Gomer. And this is Code Drakos, who's heading to Tennessee. So, now that you're all acquainted, can I get you anything?"

"No, ma'am." Seth smiled at her. Damn, she was a live wire, that one.

"No, thank you," Tyler said, his voice tight.

"We're good," Code added.

"Okay. Then off I go. I've got three more coming to check in. They'll be here any second now."

Everyone turned toward the registration desk as if they expected to see people, but there was no one at the desk ... until there was. Three people, just as Blessing had said. Yeah, woo-woo. She had to have the gift. His mom had talked about it as if it were a real thing. His father had told her she was insane, but his mom had had insights that normal people didn't. Blessing? She was freakishly gifted.

He shifted his attention to Dean, who was gripping his phone just as tight as Tyler was. "Everything all right?" Seth asked, tipping his chin toward the cell gripped in Dean's fist.

Dean grabbed his duffel and groaned aloud at the dog handler's question.

"Yeah. All good. Just my mother checking on when I'm getting in. Funny, though. That lady at the desk was dead on when she guessed it was Mom."

Noah's brow rose. "You know what's really funny? She just dumped a whole bunch of personal shit on me that was dead on, too." Seth didn't hear much more than that, but he knew exactly who they were talking about.

"You talking about Blessing?" Tyler asked.

Dean nodded, and Tyler sighed. "Yeah ... she told me ... well, just quoted some author and thought it would mean something to me. I have no clue what the hell she was referring to. Although she seemed to know why I needed to get on my flight."

Seth let out a short laugh. Man, he was right. The woman *was* a psychic or something. "No kidding. She told me the name of the vet in the town I'm going to. There are *maybe* three hundred people in that town, and she knows two of them. What are the chances of that?"

Dean widened his eyes. "So, she's like ..."

"Psychic?" Code asked.

Seth nodded. "Woo-woo." That was his word for it. Call it what you want, but that woman had it in spades.

Tyler looked at his phone. "A witch?"

They all laughed at that. Granted, it was a nervous laugh because ... yeah. Seth looked at his watch. "Gomer and I are going to take a walk so he can find some grass. We'll be back unless I get a text telling me he has to be loaded."

He stood, and Gomer was immediately at his heel. Tyler rubbed his head. "Thanks for the therapy, Gomer."

Seth smiled and grabbed his backpack just in case that text came in. "Come on, bud," he said to Gomer, and they headed out to the fresh air.

"Don't forget to say hi to my friend Kate for me," Blessing said as he walked out of the USO.

He stopped and smiled at her. "I'll be back. I'm just taking him for a comfort break."

Blessing just smiled. "Sure." She leaned down and stroked Gomer's fur. "Goodbye, Gomer. You've got a good home now," Blessing said to the dog and then winked at him before spinning around and picking up the phone. "Hello?"

He looked at Gomer. "Did that phone ring?"

The dog's head cocked as he looked at the woman. Seth shook his head. "Yeah, I didn't think so either."

Twenty minutes later, as he and Gomer reentered the terminal, his phone buzzed. It was a text from the service counter. His plane was loading for departure. He shook his head. Woo-woo didn't even scratch the surface of that woman's ability.

CHAPTER 2

Allison Sanderson no longer grimaced when Sheriff Ken Zorn's cruiser pulled up in front of her bakery. The familiar thrum of his engine didn't twist her stomach with dread the way it used to. It had been almost two years, more than that, actually, since the disaster that was their so-called on-and-off-but-mostly-off-again relationship had finally imploded.

She chuckled under her breath as she wiped down the counter, remembering the countless sessions with Dr. Wheeler. They'd tried to piece together the reasons she'd held onto Ken long after the feelings were gone. It had been a selfish kind of tethering, and she wasn't proud. If she couldn't have him, she didn't want anyone else to, either.

HOME CHANGES

The trouble was, she hadn't even wanted him.

She let him dangle, caught on the hook of her indecision, for far too long. The guilt of it had swamped her once the truth had settled in, and it was another ugly knot she'd worked out. It had taken time, but the past two years had been productive. Lonely, maybe, but as she'd discovered, growth often was.

There'd been a brief connection with a motorcycle mechanic from Rapid City. Nail had been everything she'd thought she needed. Big. Burly. Unapologetically blunt. And yet, while he had no trouble telling her exactly what he thought, their priorities had never quite lined up. And the three-hour drive between them hadn't helped.

He was a good man, and she didn't regret the time they'd spent together. But the slow, steady clarity she'd gained through her work with Dr. Wheeler had taught her that alignment mattered. It mattered more than chemistry. It mattered more than comfort.

Outside, Ken lingered on his phone before walking in, the jingle of the bell above the door pulling her from her thoughts. Allison reached beneath the counter and pulled out a brown paper bag, already packed with his usual order. She placed it on top of the display case and offered a smile.

"Hey, Ken. How's life treating you today?"

He slid off his sunglasses and tucked them into his shirt pocket. "Things are good. People are behaving themselves. No UFOs or Bigfoot sightings lately."

They both laughed, the shared amusement warm and familiar. It was an unspoken reference to Edna Michaelson, Hollister's most enthusiastic believer in all things unexplained.

Edna was a local institution. Her beliefs were as loud as her personality, and neither had ever met a boundary they respected. She butted into everyone's lives without apology and somehow managed to make people love her for it. She'd once been dubbed the town gossip and still held the title, although time and her innate kindness had softened the edges of her title. Her heart was always in the right place.

Ken tilted his head, his eyes dropping to Allison's bandaged hand. "How's your hand doing?"

She glanced down, flexing her fingers slowly. The bandage wrapped around her wound shifted as the muscles moved beneath the healing skin.

"It's doing good," she said. "There for a while, after the surgery, everything I made looked like a pile of cow dung. But it got easier once I got used to using my left hand more. Now I can use my right just as well. I go back in two days for the final follow-up and hopefully to get cleared from any restrictions."

He nodded. "That's good. That was the most excitement we've had in a while. Well, aside from the … Barry thing last year."

Allison narrowed her eyes at him, crossing her arms. "You know the entire town knows exactly what happened."

Ken shrugged, a lopsided grin tugging at the corner of his mouth. "Absolutely no comment."

It was his go-to response whenever someone mentioned the incident. Everyone in Hollister had heard something, and speculation had run rampant. Guardian Security had been involved; of that much, everyone was certain. Yet nobody spoke openly about what had gone down, and no one would.

That was the way of things in Hollister. The townspeople knew Guardian existed and that they operated out of the Marshall Ranch on the edge of town. Every person in town had some kind of connection to the ranch and understood the people who rotated through weren't just a bunch of horse trainers and ranch hands.

Allison suspected there was far more going on out there than anyone let on. She also knew better than to ask. But then again, Allison liked that there was law enforcement close by. Not that she didn't trust Ken or the work he and his deputies did. Ken Zorn was a good sheriff, steady and fair. She wouldn't take anything away from him. But knowing that when he needed backup, there were people at the Marshall Ranch who could be there in minutes?

That made life in Hollister feel a whole lot safer.

She changed the subject, tilting her head toward the large front window. "It does seem quiet today. Delbert's out front of the store without Chester. Do you know what happened to him?" Concern tugged at her expression as she turned fully to Ken. "I know he was having a hard time. Is he sick?"

Ken shook his head. "No. He's at home. Seth came back a few weeks ago.

Her brow furrowed. "Seth? His son? He was older than us, right? Sarah's brother?"

"Yeah. Only he had to make a quick trip back east. He'll be gone a couple of days," Ken explained. "Before he left, he took Chester's keys and disconnected the battery on the old tractor. There's no way for him to make it into town. Deputies swing by every two to three hours or so just to make sure he's still safe and at home."

Allison frowned. "Why would he do that? Strand his father and leave?"

Ken sighed. "You know Chester. He's always been a cantankerous old fool, but lately ... he's mean. We all saw it that day at the diner. Gen told the girls to let him know he wasn't welcome there anymore." He paused, voice quieting. "When that happened, I called Sarah. Seth was with her. He drove out here, talked to his dad, and ... well, he saw it. Realized just how bad Chester's confusion had gotten."

Allison folded her arms and bit her lower lip, gaze drifting toward the general store at the far end of the street. Chester and Delbert had been fixtures in that spot for as long as she could remember. They were always sitting on that wooden bench, solving the world's problems one comment at a time.

"It's sad, seeing them get that old," she murmured. "It just means we're getting that much older, too." Ken chuckled softly, nodding his head in agreement.

"At least you've got a family now," she added, offering a soft smile. "Congratulations, by the way. Gen told me Sam and you were adopting."

Ken's grin widened, and he slapped his palm

lightly against his thigh. "News travels faster than sunlight through a window in this town."

Allison laughed. "Well, if you're gonna tell one person, you might as well tell them all. When's the baby going to get here?"

"End of April. Maybe early May. We're doing a private adoption and it is the woman's first, so it could be a bit later than the due date." Ken said proudly. "I can tell you, I'm about as happy as I can get. I never thought I'd have a family."

A quiet pause settled between them, a shade of something unspoken stretching across the space. "Speaking of pie, I added one to your order as a congratulations." Allison sighed, her voice softer. "I'm sorry about what happened between us, Ken."

He shrugged. "That situation was two-sided. It took both of us to make that mess. You worked on you; I worked on me. I'd say that's water under the bridge. And I've told you that before. You've got to stop dragging it back up and beating yourself up over it."

Allison gave a breathy laugh. "But it's my favorite thing to beat myself up about. What will I do if I don't have that?"

Ken laughed as he reached for his wallet. "I don't

know. But you'll have to find something else to use as your lash and whip."

She rang him up for the bread and handed him his change. Ken tipped an imaginary hat, gave her a grin, then walked out to his SUV.

It was nearly one-thirty, and Allison moved into her closing routine. She wiped down all the counters and sanitized the workstations for tomorrow. Pulling a few expired items from the fridge, she dropped them into a compostable bag, then walked out the back door to toss them in the trash.

The alley was quiet. But she heard something scrape. Her head jerked toward the left.

"Hello?" she called, squinting down the narrow space between buildings. Stepping to the side, she glanced toward the front, but nothing moved. With a huff, Allison mumbled, "Could've sworn I heard someone walking." She shook her head. "Girl, you've spent so much time alone, now you're talking to yourself."

She laughed and tossed the bag into the trash can. "And now you're answering yourself. Perfect."

With that, she dropped the lid, brushed off her hands, and skipped lightly up the steps. There was still cash to count and books to balance before the day ended.

The daily total wasn't fantastic, but it wasn't catastrophic either. She'd weathered worse.

There were days she hadn't made a single sale and weeks when business had boomed unexpectedly. She was slowly learning the town's rhythm, how to gauge her customers and adjust her expectations with the seasons.

Winter was the hardest. The snow made travel difficult, and people stayed indoors. Most women baked at home during those colder months, filling their kitchens with the warmth and smells of their own homemade goods. But come summer, when the air was thick with heat and no one wanted their oven on, her sales soared. Plus, she had her regulars.

The Hollisters and the Marshalls were her backbone. The folks training at the Marshall Ranch accounted for most of her steady income. The ranch had a dining hall for them, and Allison supplied the bread, cakes, and pies. The Hollisters placed weekly orders, too, keeping their ranch hands well fed. The rest came in sporadically. Locals popping in for a muffin, a Danish, or fresh bread and soup rolls.

Her sourdough bread was a staple. People who used to buy it at the general store when she sold the bread there now strolled a little farther down the street to get it directly from her. It was a small thing, but it meant everything. She'd made something of her own. She was successful. Not rich, not by any stretch, but self-sustaining.

She made enough to pay the modest rent Mr. Hollister charged her. She covered her utilities, kept her pantry and fridge stocked with ingredients, and even managed to tuck a bit into savings.

She was comfortable. But comfort wasn't quite the same as fulfilled. Something was still missing, a quiet ache she couldn't quite name that lived deep inside her. She'd spoken to Dr. Wheeler about it more than once. He always reminded her that her future was unwritten and that anything was possible. But deep down, Allison had accepted she might spend the rest of her life single. She wasn't bitter about it. Some people just weren't meant to be attached, and she refused to wallow in self-pity.

Every weekday at two fifteen sharp, Kathy Marks jogged by the bakery. Allison joined her for their afternoon jog without fail. They'd started running together in August when Kathy had started prepping for the school year. Kathy had her last period free, and the two women had fallen into an easy routine. Allison had dropped forty pounds in the last two years, and the run was something she did for herself, too. She felt good, stronger, lighter, and for the first time, she wasn't trying to change her body to please or entice a man.

She was doing it for herself. That was liberating. And maybe, she thought with a grin, so she could justify sampling her own treats … and occasionally indulge in one of Gen Hollister's legendary cinnamon rolls.

She was halfway to the front door, keys in hand, when Edna Michaelson popped up on the boardwalk, breathless and hurrying toward the entrance. Her gray hair frizzled and flopped erratically around her face.

"Am I too late? Can I still pick up my order?"

Allison stepped back and held the door open. "Nope, you're not too late. I've got your order right here. I've already cleared out the till, but I'll add it to tomorrow's sales."

She walked behind the counter and grabbed the box she'd packed earlier: two cream horns, one sourdough baguette, and three blueberry hand pies.

Edna pulled the exact amount from her worn leather coin purse. It was the same standing order she'd picked up every week for the past year and a half.

Edna hesitated, brow knitting. "We still have an arrangement, right?"

Allison responded with a solemn nod. "No one knows what's in your order. No one needs to know." She crossed her arms over her chest. "If a lady wants a cream horn with her morning coffee, she deserves to have one."

Edna nodded, her chin lifting with pride. "You're correct. It's nobody's business."

As she took the box, she sighed heavily, and Allison tilted her head, picking up the shift in Edna's mood. "What's the matter?"

The older woman looked at her, lips pursed, like she was weighing a decision.

Allison placed her hands on her hips. "Edna Michaelson, you know you can talk to me. I haven't told a soul what's in your order for over a year. You can tell me anything."

Edna looked from left to right, then sighed heavily again. "I'm thinking about selling my place."

Allison's head snapped up, her frown forming instantly as she jerked back as if someone had physically shoved her. "What do you mean? The ranch?"

Edna nodded. "Yep. I have the small cottage here that I'm renting. That ranch house is just too darn big for me by myself. And it's getting harder and harder to make the drive in winter to check on it. Belinda's got a room for me in her house here in town, and she'd love for me to move in. Her boys are grown and out of the house, you know. But I'm just not sure I'm ready for a permanent roommate, female at least. I mean, independence is something I've fought for all my life. Maybe I could build a little house in town instead of renting." Edna shook her head. "Bah, don't let this old woman's rattling on bother you, sweetie. Thanks for the order."

"You never have to worry about talking with me, Edna. Unless it's about Bigfoot or a UFO, I won't say anything." Allison smiled at her friend.

Edna laughed. "I know what everyone thinks. You think I'm touched in the head, but I'm not. One day, I'll prove it to you." She shifted the box in her hand, and her voice softened, weighted with emotion. "You know my husband worked so hard on that place. I don't want to see it fall into disrepair. It's just a small spread. I know Mr. Hollister would buy it. Or Mr. Marshall, if I asked. But..." She shook her head slowly. "I'd kinda like to see a family there. You know what I'm saying?"

Allison did. She leaned forward, braced her hands against the glass display case, and watched Edna's face closely.

"But Kathy and Barry are settled," Edna continued, "and I don't know of any other newlyweds around here. Especially not any who could afford the place."

Allison gave her a soft smile. "Do you need to sell for financial reasons?"

Edna rolled her eyes. "Oh, heavens no. That place has been paid off forever. Taxes aren't a problem either, I've got the permanent homestead exemption." She shrugged. "It's not about the money. It's just ... It's a big house. And a lot of work." She sighed. "As I said, Belinda has room for me, and we're good enough friends." She glanced at Allison. "I'd like to keep it that way, so I'm not inclined to move in with her." She laughed and then said, "It's getting hard taking care of that big old place all by myself."

"Well, you've got plenty of time to figure it out," Allison said gently. "It's not like you're in a rush, right?"

Edna shook her head. "Nope, not at all. I just figured I'd start putting the word out, slow-like, to people who might know people. You know what I mean? I don't want this to turn into town gossip. You know how that goes." She gave Allison a pointed look. "If Chester and Delbert over there got wind I was thinking about selling, the whole town would know. And next thing you know, people'd be saying I was going crazy, or I need to be carted off to an insane asylum. You know how stories grow around here."

Allison stifled a laugh, biting the inside of her cheek. "I know exactly what you mean, Edna. Exactly."

A sharp metallic clang made them both jump. The sound of a trash can lid hitting the gravel behind the bakery echoed around the corner.

Allison lifted a finger. "Hold on, Edna. Something just knocked over my trash can."

Edna was already backing toward the door. "Oh, girl, let me get out of here. You lock up. I know you've got your run with Kathy coming up. And now, remember, don't you go spreading rumors. I'm just looking, not selling yet."

Allison chuckled. "I got you, girl. I'm not saying a word."

She followed Edna out the door, locked it behind them, and tugged the shade down to signal the bakery was closed.

Jogging back through the shop, she grabbed the old broom near the back door. If it were a groundhog, or worse, a raccoon, in her trash again, she would swat it clear to the next county.

She pushed open the door and froze.

The trash can lid lay discarded on the concrete. The bag she'd tossed in earlier, full of expired bread and pastries, was ripped open.

Carefully, Allison moved forward and peered into the can.

No raccoon. No groundhog. No critter in sight.

But the food?

Gone.

She glanced around the alley behind the store. Nothing else was missing or out of place. Nothing disturbed except the trash.

"What in the heck …" Kathy Marks jogged up just as Allison was circling the can. "You're not ready yet?" Kathy asked, slowing to a walk.

"Just give me five seconds. Edna came in late, and then I thought I had a raccoon or skunk in the trash."

Kathy took a quick step back. Then another. And another. "Raccoons and skunks? I don't deal with either."

Allison laughed, the tension easing from her shoulders. "We all remember what happened with your dogs and those skunks."

Kathy held up both hands, fingers crossed. "Not for a long time, thank God."

Allison sprinted up the back steps, tossed the broom inside, and grabbed her keys. Between the bread orders and Ken's visit, she'd already changed into her T-shirt and running shorts earlier in the afternoon.

Kathy stood by the back porch, recounting the details of a playground fight that had broken out earlier in the day.

By the time Allison had locked the back door and zipped her keys into her pocket, Kathy was still mid-story.

They took off down the street together at a comfortable jog, feet pounding the pavement in a steady rhythm.

It was just another day in paradise.

CHAPTER 3

Seth turned down the long gravel driveway that led to his childhood home. Gomer sat alert in the passenger seat, his dark gaze scanning the fields and trees as they approached the small, weathered house tucked against the edge of the property.

Damn, it hit him just how much the place needed attention. Desperately.

The white paint was peeling, flaking off in thin strips like dried leaves, and a few shingles were missing from the roof. He made a mental note to inspect the attic as soon as possible. If there was water damage up there, it could lead to a far worse problem.

Inside the house, his father had let things go. Seth

wouldn't call Chester a hoarder, but the man hadn't thrown out anything that might one day prove useful since Seth's mother had died. Stacks of cartons, bulging paper bags, old magazines, and random boxes cluttered the rooms. Bonfire fodder, all of it.

He'd work on it while he stayed with his dad. Seth had called as soon as he and Gomer landed in Rapid City to let Chester know they were on their way. Ken was stopping by later to give him a rundown on how his dad had been doing while he was gone.

As he pulled into the driveway, the front door creaked open, revealing Chester Hansen, squinting through the mesh of the screen door with his hands planted on his hips.

Seth got out and walked around the truck, letting Gomer hop down beside him. The old man watched them both with a mix of suspicion and confusion.

"What are you doing here, boy?" Chester growled, voice rough from years of hard living. "Aren't you supposed to be in the military?"

Seth kept his tone steady, patient. "No, Dad. I'm retired now. I was here just a couple of days ago, remember?"

Chester frowned, eyes narrowing. "Of course, I remember."

But Seth could tell from the blank look in his father's eyes that he didn't.

"What the hell is that?" Chester pointed toward Gomer.

"This is my military working dog. He's retired now, so he'll be staying here with us."

"Dogs don't belong in the house," Chester snapped. "You can put him out in the barn."

"Dad, this one belongs in the house. He's a drug detection dog and one of the best trackers in Europe."

Chester crossed his arms and looked down at Gomer, who sat calmly beside Seth, his ears forward, posture obedient and proud.

"Then why the hell ain't it in Europe?"

"He's got some arthritis. They're putting him out to pasture because he's slowed down."

Chester's arms fell to his sides as he stared at the dog. His voice dropped, quieter now. "They do that to dogs and humans. Slow down, and the world just forgets about you. Leaves you behind. What's his name?"

"Gomer."

Chester snorted. "What in the name of muddy water would you call a dog that for?"

Seth grinned, remembering having the same thought when he'd first heard the name.

"I didn't name him, Dad. The Air Force did."

"Well, then, the Air Force is stupider than muddy water."

"If you say so, Pops."

"Well, I do," Chester muttered, then added, "I suppose you want me to be nice to it now, don't you?"

Seth nodded once. "Well, sir, I would appreciate it."

Chester reached down and gave Gomer a rough pat on the head. "Come on. I'm hungry. You probably could do with a bite." He cast a look back over his shoulder at Seth. "You can fix your own food."

Seth rubbed the back of his neck and laughed. "Yes, sir. I'll do that."

He grabbed his backpack and the large bag of dog food he'd picked up in Rapid City, slinging both over his shoulder. Once inside, he dropped them near the entryway and headed for the kitchen, where he froze in the doorway.

Chester was sitting at the table, breaking off

chunks of sharp cheddar and feeding them to Gomer one piece at a time.

"Dad, I've got dog food for him. You're gonna spoil him giving him people food."

"You said he was put out to pasture," Chester said without looking up. "Seems to me that pasture ought to be lush. All us old cantankerous farts want a lush pasture. Whether we get it or not."

Seth rolled his eyes. "Just don't give him too much of that, Dad. I don't want him to get sick."

Chester reached for another piece of cheese. "No promises. You just go tend to you," Chester said, waving Seth off like he didn't have a care in the world. "I've had dogs before. I know how much is too much."

Seth didn't argue. He knew better than to push when his father had that look in his eye.

He went to the sink, turned on the faucet, and washed his hands. Through the window, he caught sight of Ken's cruiser easing down the gravel drive.

"Dad," he called over his shoulder, "Ken's coming down the drive. I'm gonna go see what he needs."

Chester didn't respond, just waved one hand in a dismissive circle as he continued breaking the cheese into small chunks, popping one into his mouth, then giving one to Gomer.

Seth shook his head. At this rate, Gomer would need double his exercise. Too much weight on a dog with arthritis wasn't just uncomfortable; it was dangerous.

Ken parked in front of the house and stepped out of his SUV, nodding a greeting as Seth came outside. "He was fine every time someone came to check on him," Ken said, reaching out to shake Seth's hand. "Got angry at us for disturbing his peace, though." He chuckled. "He's doing better now. Not as mean. For a while there, I wasn't sure what was going on."

Seth leaned against the SUV, arms crossed over his chest. "He forgot I came home. Asked me why I was back and thought I was still in the military. I'll take him to Belle Fourche and get him a full physical. Make sure we know where we're starting from. I've been reading about treatment options. Some meds can help clear the fog a bit."

Ken nodded slowly. "I know this has to be hard on you."

Seth exhaled through his nose. "I never thought I'd see the day Chester Hansen wasn't in full control of everything around him." He hesitated, then added, "I'll need to find a lawyer, too. I talked to Dad a few days ago, during a lucid moment. He doesn't have a will. No power of attorney. Nothing is set up for medical or financial decisions."

"My wife's a lawyer. Family law," Ken offered.

Seth frowned. "Allison's a lawyer? I didn't know that."

Ken burst out laughing. "I'm not married to Allison. My wife's name is Sam. She was a state patrol officer before she became a lawyer. Runs a small family practice right here in Hollister. She stays busy writing cattle contracts in the slow season and takes on pro bono cases, too. We're expecting our first, adopting a baby actually, and we think she'll be here in April next year."

"Holy crap, congratulations, man." Seth extended his hand and shook Ken's. The pride in his expression was priceless.

"Thanks, man. We're really happy." He added, "So, if you're worried you can't afford to get everything squared away for Chester, she can work something out with you."

Seth shook his head. "I'm not worried about the money, Ken. I saved and invested pretty well during my time in the military. I've got a solid retirement. For what little we need up here, I can take care of Dad and me for a while. At least until he needs to go into a facility."

Ken didn't sugarcoat it. "That's gonna suck."

"It will indeed," Seth agreed, his voice quiet. Pausing, he tilted his head slightly. "So ... you didn't marry Allison? How did that not happen? You two dated forever."

Ken gave a slow smile. "That's a long story. One of those you tell over a cold adult beverage." Ken grinned. "Come to dinner sometime. Sam and I would love to have you over, and we'll catch you up on all the town's comings and goings."

Seth reached out and shook his hand. "Sounds like a plan. Just let me know when and where."

Behind them, the screen door creaked open, and Gomer trotted outside and came straight to Seth, sitting neatly at his heel, tongue lolling and eyes bright.

Ken looked down. "And who is this?"

Before Seth could answer, Chester shuffled onto the porch.

"That is Gomer," he said, pointing with one hand. "He got put out to pasture. Just like me."

Seth chuckled, patting Gomer's head. "He's my military working dog. I adopted him after we both retired."

Ken frowned and looked at Seth with a raised brow. "You were a dog handler?"

Seth nodded. "More than that. Started as a handler, then trainer, and moved up to kennel master. Eventually, I ran the MWD Major Command program. Mostly pushing paper. I hated it. Took me away from the dogs."

Ken lifted an eyebrow, considering that. "Good to know. Real good to know." He glanced toward his cruiser, then back at Seth. "Well, let me know if you need anything. And, Chester, don't forget about the Fall Festival next month."

Seth glanced toward the house. "What's that?"

He looked at his father, who just blinked at him.

"Hell if I know," Chester grumbled. "What do I look like, Hollister Social Services?"

Ken stopped mid-step and stared at Chester, baffled. Then he shook his head. "Chester, you know everything about everything that happens in this town."

Chester shrugged. "Don't know nothing about no stupid festival." With that, he turned around and shuffled back into the house, muttering under his breath.

Ken watched him go, mouth twitching with disbelief. "I've been in five or six conversations where your father talked about that festival."

Seth nodded. "Figured as much."

Ken let out a slow breath. "Well, just so you know, Declan Howard owns the Bit and Spur now, and he built a community center onto the back of it."

"I noticed there was a big addition," Seth said. "Didn't realize it was a community space."

Ken nodded. "Yeah. We do barbecues, festivals, and town gatherings. A couple of wedding receptions, Christmas dances. That kind of thing. Gives folks something to look forward to. We're putting together a Fall Festival for mid-October. Pumpkins, haystacks, and wagon rides for the kids. Community barbecue. It's taken over." Ken sighed. "Flyers all over town, and all the businesses are supporting it. Well, most of it. Someone mentioned a greased pig contest," Ken added with a laugh. "But I think that got nixed. The new vet was ready to strangle the guys who suggested it."

"That's Tegan's new wife, right?"

Ken nodded. "Yeah, you know Tegan, don't you?"

Seth shrugged. "All of y'all were a couple of years younger than me. But I remember Tegan. Quiet guy."

"Still is. But his wife?" Ken whistled low. "She's not quiet. Former Army. Smart, tough, and not afraid to speak her mind. And frankly, she's exactly what this town needs. Doc Macy's only doing large animals now, and Kate handles the small ones."

"I'll need to set up an appointment," Seth said, glancing down at Gomer, who had settled at his feet. "I've got his full medical records. She'll have a solid base to work from."

"Not sure you need an appointment. Most people just pull up. Her office is at the stockyard where Tegan works. How bad is the dog's arthritis?"

Seth lifted a shoulder. "Well, if he were still working, it'd be bad enough to be a problem. He couldn't deploy. It's tough to medicate a working dog in the field, so they pulled him. Gave him an honorable retirement. He'll have a long, happy life here. He's eight now, so I figure I've got four or five good years left with him."

"That was good of you, taking him in."

"You don't get it." Seth shook his head. "It was good of the Air Force to give him to me." Ken looked confused. Seth crouched slightly, resting a hand on Gomer's back as the dog leaned into his leg. "I've made attachments to five or six dogs over the years. You work with them, trust them with your life ... It's a bond. I knew Gomer when he first came to the kennel as a green dog. I was managing the kennel at the base level. I kept track of him even after I promoted myself out of that job.

"I've got a buddy, Reid, who feeds me info about

the MWDs getting retired. Who's going home and who's getting put down." Seth's voice tightened. "I made a few calls when I saw Gomer on that list. There was no reason to euthanize him. He's friendly, stable. Still got so much life left in him. So, I pushed, and I got my dog." He reached down and rubbed the tops of Gomer's ears gently. The dog closed his eyes and pressed closer.

"Even if I'm not working a dog, I need one around. In the military, I couldn't. Too many logistics, too many moves. But now I can. Where I go, Gomer goes."

Ken watched the pair, something quiet passing behind his expression. Then he straightened and gave Seth a nod. "Well, I'd better get out and make my rounds. I've gotta run out to the Marshall Ranch and see Frank for a few minutes." He paused. "You do realize Frank Marshall has ties to Guardian Security, right?"

Seth lifted an eyebrow. "No. Why should I? It's not like I've been back for anything other than Mom's funeral."

Ken shrugged. "Just a comment in passing. Hell, everyone knows it, even if no one in this town would ever admit to it. We take care of our own around here, Seth. And this town? It's growing, mostly because of the Hollisters and the Marshalls. We're in a bit of a boom right now. I don't know what's gonna happen when the economy takes a dive, but I've seen this little town stretched thin. People pulled together to make sure no one went hungry. That's who we are. Right now, we don't have to do that. And we've got those two ranching families to thank for it. So, yeah, we take care of our own."

Seth tilted his head slightly. "Is that a warning?"

Ken barked out a laugh. "Warning? Hell no. Just a bored sheriff talking to someone who ain't been around in a while. That's all." He gave a short nod and headed back to his cruiser. "I'll let you go, but don't forget about the Fall Festival. You'll see flyers at the diner or in Allison's bakery. Mrs. Sanderson's General Store expanded a little. You can get most of what you need there. But if you need to stay close to home with Chester, just ask around. There's always someone making a run to Belle or Rapid. You need something we don't have up here, someone'll grab it for you."

"It's just like it used to be, just with a few more people now," Seth said.

"Yup." Ken climbed into his SUV and started it up. He leaned out the window before backing out.

"You take care of yourself and that old man of yours."

His eyes dropped to Gomer, who stood at Seth's side like a statue.

"And you … You take care of them all."

Seth waved as Ken backed out, made a slow three-point turn, and headed down the long driveway toward the road. As the cruiser disappeared over the ridge, Seth looked down at the dog beside him.

"Yep," he muttered, scratching behind Gomer's ear. "Some things never change."

CHAPTER 4

Allison closed her eyes as the physician assistant gently pulled the final staple from her incision. It didn't hurt. But watching it happen? That was another matter.

She wasn't squeamish by nature, and she could handle herself in a crisis, but blood, especially her own, made her stomach wobble just a little too easily. She cracked one eye open, then the other, catching the wide, amused smile on the PA's face. Allison rolled her eyes toward the ceiling. "Sorry. I get queasy."

The woman patted her gently on the leg. "Not a problem. You're good to go now. The doctor looked over the x-rays. Everything's healing beautifully. If you have any problems at all, just give us a call.

Honestly, I'm surprised by how much mobility you already have. Most people who follow physical therapy to the letter don't progress this fast."

Allison hopped down from the exam table smoothly, landing lightly on her feet.

"Well, I didn't exactly follow the prescribed PT." She gave a sheepish grin. "I own and run a bakery. Kneading dough, shaping bread, carrying heavy trays, it was all built-in therapy. When I looked at the exercises, I figured I was already doing most of them, just a lot more reps."

The PA blinked, her mouth falling open slightly.

"You mean to tell me you've been using that hand to knead bread this whole time, and you haven't had any issues?"

Allison shook her head. "No, none. I put on a glove and worked. Not much else I could've done. That bakery is my livelihood. Don't get me wrong, it ached for quite a while. It was a pain in the butt, but I took some Tylenol and kept going. The first two weeks? Oh my goodness, my bread looked awful. I gave the practice ones to the local diner to use for toast. I wasn't about to sell them."

She laughed softly, remembering the mess.

"My mom helped me with orders, but I had nothing in the display case for at least two weeks.

After that, though, I adapted. The more I worked, the more I could work."

The PA shook her head with what looked like admiration. "I wish more patients were like you. Some people get injured and never put in the effort to rebuild the muscle. They lose mobility just because they give up too early. I'm so glad you didn't."

Allison lifted her hand and flexed her fingers, giving a small, confident wiggle. There was no pain, no weakness. "Nope. The doctor did a great job. I'm fine."

"You are indeed," the PA said with a smile. "It's been a pleasure meeting you, Allison. And I hope I never see you again."

Allison grinned and reached out to shake her hand. "Same to you. But if you're ever up in Hollister, stop by the bakery. I'll give you a sample of something sweet."

"Hollister?" the woman asked with a laugh. "That's a long way north. I think I'm staying right here ... maybe wander down to Rapid City. No plans to head north anytime soon. But if I do, I'll let you know."

Allison waved goodbye and left the exam room. She stopped at the nurses' desk to ensure her copay was handled and her insurance information was complete. Satisfied, she walked down the long, tiled hallway, her purse slung over her shoulder.

As she approached the glass double doors at the end of the corridor, she saw a man standing outside.

She slowed, a frown pulling at her brow.

She knew him.

Didn't she?

Then it clicked.

Seth. Seth Hansen.

She remembered him as clearly as if it were yesterday. He'd been a senior when she was a freshman, a big, strong ranch kid, starting defense and offense, the cornerstone of their thirteen-man football team. Big. Broad. Quiet. And, from a freshman girl's perspective, utterly unreachable. She didn't remember if he'd dated much. But if he had, none of the cheerleaders had claimed him, though if memory served, they'd all tried.

He'd always seemed ... above it all.

And now, he was standing right there, just beyond the doors.

She ducked her head quickly and kept walking. She wasn't about to say anything. He probably didn't even remember her. Besides, she was taking time for herself. Healing. Or so she kept reminding herself. Two years and counting.

Allison pressed the door's metal bar, stepped outside, and let the fresh air hit her skin as she adjusted the strap on her purse. She didn't look left or right. It would be embarrassing to say hi to him and have him not know who the hell she was. Allison headed out to her truck, flexing her hand, glad the staples were gone.

Behind her, a voice called out. "Allison? Allison Sanderson?"

She stopped mid-step and turned. Seth Hansen stood behind her, tall, broad, and familiar in a way that made her chest flutter. Only this version of Seth was rugged, handsome, and not a teenager anymore. *Wowza, so not a teenager.*

She smiled. "Hey, Seth. Long time no see."

He let out a laugh, the sound low and surprised. "Over twenty years."

"As I said … a long time." Her smile widened, a little shy but genuine. "How have you been?"

"I've been good. Did my twenty-two in the military, and now, I'm back. Because, well," he glanced off to the side, "I'm sure you know. Dad's failing."

Allison's smile faltered. "Yeah … we all know about Chester. It came on slow, but it was hard to miss. It got pretty rough there for a while. He and Barry butted heads a lot. They might've come to blows if it hadn't been for Kathy. Kathy Marks. You might remember her?"

He nodded. "Vaguely."

She sighed. "Barry has, or I guess I should say had, a temper. But you'll hear about that the first time you talk to Edna Michaelson."

Seth laughed, resting his hands on his hips. "Is Edna still the town gossip?"

"Well, for the women, yes. Used to be your dad and Delbert were the ones spreading the men's gossip. Somehow, whatever Edna knew, your dad and Delbert found out within hours. There are no secrets."

"Doesn't sound like that's changed much."

"Nope. Still the same."

He smiled down at the pavement, then glanced back up at her, brow lifting slightly.

"So ... why are you here? I mean, at the hospital?"

She lifted her wrist and held it up so he could see the faint red line of the incision. "Never tangle with a broken jelly jar. It never ends well."

Seth winced. "How bad was it?"

"Bad enough that Zeke Johnson, the doctor in Hollister, wouldn't touch it. He sent me here to the hand surgeon. They say I'm healed and can do whatever I want now. But if I have any problems, I'm supposed to come back. You here with your dad?"

Seth nodded slowly. "Yeah. I probably should've been here last week, but I had to go pick up my partner."

Allison blinked. Her brain filled in the blanks. A partner. Oh.

Oh.

Well. That explained why he'd never dated in high school. He was gay. She was so slow. How had she never guessed?

"Well, I'd like to meet him," she said with a smile. "Maybe you two could stop by the bakery sometime."

Seth's brow furrowed. "You let dogs in the bakery?"

Her smile froze. "Why would you call your partner a dog? That's ... that's rude."

Maybe he wasn't just gay. Maybe he was rude, too. That would be a shame. But twenty-two years could change a person. God knew she'd changed.

"Allison," Seth said slowly, "my partner is a German Shepherd. An actual dog."

Allison felt her face flush in a hot wave of embarrassment. "Oh. You mean ... he's not a man. You're not ... gay?"

Seth's mouth dropped open for a second, then snapped shut. "What are you talking about?"

"I thought ... when you said you had to go pick up your partner ... I just assumed—"

"No," he said with a chuckle. "My partner is a military working dog. I'm a retired MWD handler. I adopted him because they took him out of service for arthritis."

Her mouth formed a silent O. Then she burst out laughing. "Oh my God. Okay. Okay. Can we start over?" She knew her face was turning a brilliant red. The heat on her cheeks had nothing to do with the late afternoon sun shining on the entrance to the hospital.

Seth was laughing, too, now, rubbing the back of his neck.

"Yeah. I'd like that. And just for the record, I'm not gay. Not even a little bit. I'm surprised you and Ken never got together," he added, studying her. "I thought for sure you two would end up married."

Allison blinked again, caught completely off guard. "How did you know ..."

"Ken and I have caught up since I've been home."

"Wow. Okay, well ... I'm surprised you even

remembered me. You were the football star. I was the dorky redhead with freckles. I was just a freshman. You were every girl's dream."

A slow smile crept across Seth's face. "Even yours?"

She lifted a brow, trying to play it cool. "Wouldn't you like to know?"

"I would," he said, voice quiet and sincere. "Always thought you were the cutest thing in Hollister."

Her mouth parted slightly. Words failed her. Had she heard that right? She pointed to herself. "Me?"

Seth looked around the nearly empty hospital entryway. "I don't see anyone else standing here. Of course, you."

Allison shrugged, a touch of color rising in her cheeks. "Uh ... thanks for the compliment?"

Just then, Seth's phone vibrated. He pulled it from his pocket, glanced at the screen, and then tucked it away again with a sigh.

"The nurse says Dad's doctor is ready to talk to us. He's inside watching the news. I had to get out for a minute. Hospitals kinda make me go stir-crazy."

"What's he here for?" Allison asked, and before he could answer, she added, "You do know we have a doctor in Hollister now, right? Zeke Johnson? I told you that. We even have a psychiatrist, Dr. Wheeler."

Seth nodded. "Yeah. A friend suggested a full physical wouldn't be a bad idea. I'm swimming upstream with him most days, so I figured I'd get him assessed while I still could. His insurance and Medicare cover it, so why not? Plus, this doctor specializes in dementia and Alzheimer's cases. I figured we should get ahead of it if we can."

"Oh, that's a good idea," she said, softening at the mention of that terrible disease. There was an awkward pause before she slid a step toward her truck. "Well ... I'll let you get back inside, Seth. You should stop by sometime. The bakery's open until two, Monday through Saturday. Unless I'm in Belle Fourche for an appointment."

"I'll make it a point to stop by ... with my partner." He winked at her. She blinked and blinked again. A smile spread across his face. "See you, Allison."

She smiled and waved ... like a dork. "See you later, Seth."

Turning, Allison made her way back to her truck, her thoughts tangled with the last few minutes.

One of the cutest girls in Hollister. I'll make it a point to stop by. Why? What? Had he really said that?

She couldn't remember his exact words anymore, and maybe she'd imagined it. Or misheard him.

But no ...

No, he had said it.

She bit her lip and glanced back toward the hospital doors he'd just walked through. Did she really need this kind of confusion in her life right now? She let out a low laugh, shaking her head. Of course not. Nothing would come of this. Things like this never happened in her life. Still ... She took a deep breath, smiled to herself, and accepted the compliment for what it was. It was *nice*. And maybe ... just maybe, it meant a little more than nothing. She would wait and see.

CHAPTER 5

Seth sat stiffly in the corner of the exam room, arms crossed, his spine ramrod straight. His gut was clenched tight.

The last time he and his father had been in a hospital room together, Seth had been the one in the bed. Sixteen years old, stitched up and bruised, nursing injuries that came from trouble he had no business being in. Chester hadn't said much back then. He'd stood in the doorway, jaw tight, arms crossed. He knew his father was pissed. His dad was always pissed at him for one thing or another. Seth had never won his dad's praise. Never measured up. The silent condemnation was a constant for as long as Seth could remember. Yeah, no words were necessary in their relationship.

This time, he'd royally messed up, though. It wasn't

chores that weren't done to Chester's standards or grades that weren't perfect, and it wasn't that he didn't move fast enough when his mom asked him to help out. No, this time, he'd outright disobeyed his dad. He'd fixed up the old truck Chester had given him. Worked damn hard to get it running, and against his dad's wishes, he'd taken it to the homecoming party at the lake. The parking brake failed, and he'd tried his hardest to keep it from rolling into the water. The damn thing gained momentum, and he'd lost his footing, slipped under the front wheel, and was run over. It was funny to all the kids around him until it wasn't. Because alcohol was involved, people scattered. Gregg Koehler went to the nearest ranch and called for help. He came back and stayed with Seth until the sheriff and Chester arrived. Seth begged Gregg to leave, but he wouldn't, even though they both knew Gregg's dad would beat the tar out of him for being at the party.

Chester didn't say a word. That look and the silence did more than words or, in Gregg's case, fists, could do. Seth hated that Gregg had to pay for his mess up. When his friend showed up at the hospital three days later, the bruises and split lip told him just how much his friendship had cost Gregg. Chester stood up, walked over to Gregg, tilted his chin up, and narrowed his eyes. "Your pap do this?" he asked.

Gregg nodded.

"For helping Seth when he screwed up?"

Gregg nodded again. Chester turned and stared at Seth, lifting his finger and pointing at Gregg. No words. Seth knew exactly what Chester meant. If he'd listened, he wouldn't be in the hospital, and Gregg's dad wouldn't have laid a hand on his friend. That single movement crushed him in a way nothing else could. His father dropped his arm, shook his head, and left the room. Seth knew at that moment he'd never be enough for his dad.

Chester's disappointment was a constant in his life. It was almost as if he expected Seth to mess up. Which he did ... sometimes. But mostly that disappointment put Seth on the road out of Hollister. He knew he was meant for more, and he knew the constant disappointment he lived under wasn't who he was. That was why he'd joined the Air Force and probably why he'd excelled. The determination to prove he was better than his old man thought he was.

Not much had changed. Only now, Chester sat on the edge of the exam table, his shoulders slumped forward, hands worrying the bill of his old feed store cap like it might hold answers to questions neither of them wanted to ask.

Seth really wished it did.

The doctor had been kind and gentle yet thorough when working with his dad. She walked them through what she called a routine cognitive screening. The questions sounded simple ... until Seth had to watch his father struggle.

"What year is it, Mr. Hansen?"

Chester squinted at the ceiling, breathing hard through his nose. "Two thousand ... and ... twelve." His voice cracked.

Seth didn't move. Didn't blink. He wanted to correct him so badly it hurt. Wanted to say *Come on, Dad. You know this. How can you not know what year it is?*

But he stayed quiet. It was the hardest thing he'd ever done.

The doctor nodded and scribbled something onto her chart without missing a beat. They moved on. The clock test. Chester passed that one. The three-word memory test: apple, table, penny. His dad couldn't recall any of them when asked. They took a short walk down the hall so she could observe his gait. Blood was drawn. Vitals were checked. A CT scan was ordered.

Chester hadn't liked any of it, but to his credit, he'd gone along. *That,* more than anything, scared Seth. Chester Hansen didn't *let* people do things. He sure as hell didn't comply without argument.

All those questions. The memory games. The

scans. The medical terms. Not once was the word dementia said. Not once. But Seth could feel it. It hung in the air, thick and heavy, like smoke wafting through every breath. Everyone in the room seemed to ignore it, but it was there.

Afterward, Seth lingered in the hallway while the nurse walked Chester out to the lobby with a paper cup of water and a soft promise: *"It'll only be a few more minutes."*

The exam room door closed with a soft, final click. The quiet settled around Seth like a trap. The humming overhead lights, the faint scent of antiseptic and burned coffee, and a silence that weighed more than it should have.

The doctor returned a few moments later. She was in her fifties, with warm, perceptive eyes and a voice that cut clean through the noise without ever raising in volume. She sat across from him in a rolling chair, no computer, no tablet. Just a plain manila folder resting in her hands.

"Seth, thank you for staying," she said gently. "I wanted a moment to speak with you alone."

He nodded, jaw so tight it ached from being clenched all afternoon. "Yeah. Of course."

He braced himself. Every part of him was waiting

for the hit. She opened the folder, glanced down briefly, then looked up and met his gaze.

"We're not finished yet. There are still blood test results pending, and we'll need to review the CT scan before confirming anything officially. But …" She pulled another sheet of paper from the folder. "Based on today's cognitive screening, our clinical interview, and what you've shared with us," she paused, "your father is showing signs consistent with moderate dementia. Most likely Alzheimer's."

The words were clear. Gentle. Carefully chosen. And they hit like a fucking draft horse kick to the gut. Seth swallowed hard. "So … this isn't just him forgetting where he put his keys." He shook his head and lifted a hand. "No, don't answer that. I know it's not." He shook his head. "You're going to think this is stupid, but I was hoping that maybe it was something else. Hoping for a miracle, you know, because that isn't my dad, and … well, I'm not going to lie, the road ahead scares the heck out of me."

The doctor gave him a soft, sad smile. "It isn't stupid. Everyone in your situation likely hopes and prays for a miracle, but you're right. This won't be easy. I understand the fear of the unknown. Unfortunately, you'll need to walk that road with him because what he's dealing with is beyond normal aging. He's confused about time, place, and the sequence of events. His ability to problem solve is impaired. You witnessed that yourself today. And you said he left the stove on twice since you've been home? How long have you been staying with him?"

Seth closed his eyes and nodded, then opened them to meet the doctor's gaze.

"Almost two weeks. It took a while to get in to see you," he murmured.

"That's understandable," she said gently. "He'll need supervision ... more structure in his schedule. A routine will help. However, he'll likely need assistance with daily tasks. More than someone just checking in on him now and then." She paused. "Are you staying with him currently?"

"Yes." Seth nodded once, steady and resolute. "Until he needs more than I can give." His sister Sarah had a family counting on her in Aberdeen. He had no ties except Gomer. He'd stay.

The doctor studied him for a beat, then gave a small nod. "Does he have his legal paperwork in order? Medical power of attorney, end-of-life directives?"

"Not yet, ma'am. I just got home. The physical was the priority. However, I'll be meeting with a lawyer in Hollister to finalize everything. We'll make sure he's aware of what's happening before he signs anything. She's a court officer, so I'm sure she'll arrange for witnesses to confirm he's lucid and understands what he's signing."

"Good," the doctor said. "There are some medications that may help manage the symptoms. Maybe even slow the progression a little. We'll go over options once all the test results are in." She leaned forward slightly, her voice soft but unwavering as she continued, "But you need to understand something, Seth. This is a progressive illness. It *will* get worse. Not overnight, of course, but gradually, steadily. You'll see him slip. Sometimes the slips will be grand, sometimes it will be little things."

Seth turned his head, staring hard at the whiteboard on the wall behind her desk. It was covered in clips of articles and hospital posters, but none of it offered a miracle.

"Ma'am ... he's always been so damn stubborn," Seth said, his voice low. "Never asked for help. Never let me in. I pray that changes."

The doctor offered him a quiet, sympathetic smile. "That might not change. But how *you* respond, well, that's what matters. And you're already doing the right thing by bringing him in."

Seth nodded, emotion thick in his throat. At least

he'd done this one thing right. "Okay, what happens now?"

"We'll schedule a follow-up. My nurse will give you an information packet with helpful resources. And if you need help navigating any of it, just let us know." She rested her hand over the folder. "You're not alone in this, Seth."

He stood slowly, his body stiff with the weight of reality settling into his bones. "Thank you, ma'am. For everything." He opened the exam room door and stepped into the hallway.

There, just outside, Chester sat with his legs crossed, staring out the window like nothing had changed.

But for Seth ... everything had.

Outside, Seth walked beside his father, their steps slow as they made their way to the truck. Chester shuffled more than he walked, muttering about the fluorescent lights inside the clinic giving him a headache.

"You did good today, Dad," Seth said quietly.

Chester grunted. "Felt like a damn lab rat."

Seth tried to laugh, but it didn't quite land.

He unlocked the truck and waited as his father climbed in. The old man's joints creaked louder than the hinges on the door. Seth had come home to help, *not* to take over. But now? Now, he understood. The man who'd once seemed carved from granite was crumbling, seemingly softening into sand. And all the resentment, the lost time, the unsaid words, the silence that had stretched between them like a canyon, it all felt meaningless.

None of it mattered anymore.

Not now.

They drove home in silence. Not the angry kind. Not the cold, resentful kind either. This was the quiet of understanding. The tired kind. The kind that filled the truck cab like a fog. It was heavy with the weight of everything unspoken between them. And for Seth, at least, there was a fear that there might not be time to say it, or if he did … would his dad remember?

When they pulled into the drive, Chester opened the door and climbed out.

Seth watched him head toward the porch and called after him. "Watch the step, Dad."

"I built this damn step," Chester muttered as he took it slowly, gripping the railing harder than he needed to.

Seth didn't argue. He just stood nearby, quiet, watching the stiffness in his father's movements.

Inside, Gomer greeted him at the door, tail

sweeping the floor like a broom. Seth opened the door and let the dog outside to relieve himself, the screen door creaking shut behind him.

The house smelled like old furniture, dust, and yesterday's coffee. He'd cleaned up the stacks of stuff, well … mostly. The clutter was gone from the living room, boxes cleared and stacked in the storage shed out back. He'd moved the recliner closer to the window so Chester could sit and watch the pasture in the afternoons.

The fridge was stocked with simple meals, most of them bought at the diner after Ken's recommendation. Seth sighed, rubbing the back of his neck as he looked around.

He didn't know what he was doing. Not really. But he'd done his best and would keep doing just that.

Chester shuffled out of the hallway and paused, taking in the space like he was a guest in someone else's home. His eyes roamed the room, a faint frown pulling at his weathered face.

"Something's missing," he muttered.

"No, Pops. I just cleared some space," Seth replied gently. "Thought I'd make things easier."

Chester snorted. "Looks like a retirement home."

He made his way to the recliner and sank into it

with a long, bone-deep sigh. Within minutes, his eyes slipped shut. Seth hadn't even had time to offer him dinner.

He stood there for a moment, unmoving, watching the man who'd once walked fence lines in January without flinching. The man who'd used to yell loud enough to rattle the windows. Now, he was slumped in his chair, dozing before the sun set.

The lines on Chester's face were deep, his jaw soft, slack with exhaustion. Seth stepped quietly into the kitchen and rubbed a hand over his face, bracing himself against the counter.

If this was hard for him …

My God.

How hard was it for his father?

CHAPTER 6

*A*llison and Kathy's feet kept a steady rhythm on the gravel road, their shoes crunching against the dirt as they jogged along the familiar path just outside town. The September afternoon was hotter than usual. Some days, the run came easy. Today wasn't one of them. Allison's thoughts kept drifting back to her unexpected encounter with Seth Hansen. No matter how she tried to focus on her breathing or the trail ahead, her mind circled back to the way he'd looked at her ... and what he'd said.

One of the cutest girls in school.

She couldn't help it. The comment had burrowed under her skin, poking at places she hadn't let herself feel in years. And deep down, she knew better. She was setting herself up for disappointment. Kathy glanced over as they ran.

"Okay, girl. Spill it. What's got you all tangled up today?"

Allison glanced sideways but didn't answer right away. "You have to swear not to tell anyone," she said. "And that includes Barry."

Kathy's expression turned dead serious. "Allison Sanderson, you know for a fact I have *never* repeated anything we talk about on these runs. This is our time. It's my therapy."

Allison nodded. "Yeah, I know. I just had to lead off with that." She drew in a breath. "Seth Hansen was at the hospital in Belle Fourche yesterday."

They turned the corner that led back toward town, gravel popping underfoot. Soon they'd be behind the bakery, finishing their usual loop.

Kathy rolled her hand in a gesture for more. "You're leaving me hanging here."

Allison let out a soft laugh. "We talked for a few minutes. His dad's getting evaluated for possible dementia. We've all seen how far Chester's slipped from who he used to be."

Kathy nodded. "Yeah, I know." Their steps filled the silence for half a minute, the cadence of movement filling the space between thoughts.

Allison finally spoke again. "When we were talking ... he made a comment. He said I was one of the cutest girls at school."

Kathy's head snapped around. Her smile bloomed instantly. "Oh, man. That is *so* sweet. Is he married? Dating? Does he have someone?"

"Stop it," Allison groaned. "You and I both know I'm a magnet for complicated situations."

"Yeah, and I also know you and Doc Wheeler have been working through that." Kathy gave her a pointed look. "I don't think you understand how attractive you are. You've got a lot to bring to a relationship."

"Nobody said anything about a relationship," Allison said, fighting the urge to roll her eyes. She kept her footing steady on the gravel instead. "Seriously. It was just a comment. I probably won't even see him again for a couple of weeks. He's focused on getting his dad's medical care in place. After that? Who knows. He left over twenty years ago, and now he's only back because Chester's sick. Why would he stay?" She shook her head. "No. I'm not getting my hopes up. If we become friends, cool. But I'm not looking for a relationship. Even if the compliment really threw me."

Kathy shot her a curious look. "What do you mean it *threw* you?"

"For one, I wasn't a cute girl. You know that. You went to school with me."

Kathy made a sound of disbelief. "Are you joking? I would've killed to have your skin tone, your eyes, and that auburn hair. Girl, do you know how rare it is for someone to have *green eyes* and *red hair*? Nobody has that. Maybe two or three percent of the world's population. And you're one of them." She gave Allison a look. "You're gorgeous. Why do you think Ken stayed hooked so long?"

"Because I was a raging bitch," Allison said with a grin. "And I played him like a violin."

Kathy burst out laughing. "Well, that, too. But something had to keep his attention, and it sure wasn't your attitude." Kathy nudged her. "It was you. You've lost forty pounds, you're toned, you're beautiful, and you have long dark red hair I'd *kill* for." She gave a mock-sinister look. "Okay, maybe not kill. But I'd definitely slap someone real hard for it."

Allison couldn't help but laugh. "You're right. Not the pretty thing ... It's just that I don't see myself that way. It's been a long time since I really *looked* at myself. I wash my face, throw my hair in a ponytail, and go to work. That's about it."

Kathy smirked. "Yeah? When was the last time you put on makeup and a dress?"

"Not since I went out with Nail." She frowned as she thought about it. "Yeah, sadly, that's the last time," Allison said, her breath steadying as their pace slowed. "I'm comfortable in my own skin now. I don't need makeup at the bakery or out running with you. My self-worth doesn't revolve around who I'm dating, or not dating, for that matter." She exhaled a little harder as if saying it out loud solidified it more. "I've learned some hard lessons. And I'm accepting why I was a raving bitch, and I know how not to do that anymore. Thank God. Ken's forgiven me. Sam, well, Sam is a sweetheart, and I genuinely like her, but I still feel awkward around her. Because she knows exactly who I was and how I treated him. Hell, the entire town knows what a bitch I was."

"Girl, everyone has a past and a history. Besides, you said Doc Wheeler told you it was because of your insecurities." Kathy nudged her a bit with her elbow as they jogged.

"Which is true, but looking back, man, I played Ken like a yo-yo." She'd pulled the roots of her problem out of the ground and examined them with Dr. Wheeler. She'd been teased for being a ginger and shy when she was young. On summer vacations with her extended family, her cousins had teased her mercilessly, to the point of cruelty. When Allison had told on them, they'd deny it. It was why she wasn't close with her father's side of the family. Growing up, that insecurity grew and festered with any criticism from other kids, teachers, or adults. She adapted to it by controlling Ken because while she didn't want *him*, he wanted *her*, and his need temporarily filled the black hole of her insecurities.

"And you need to forgive yourself for it, but that will come with time."

"Damn, you been taking psych classes?" Allison laughed.

"Maybe." Kathy flicked her wrist. "Or maybe I learned it from a certain handsome ranch hand I absolutely love."

They slowed to a walk as they reached the edge of the block and circled around behind the bakery.

Allison's eyes narrowed as she spotted the trash can again. The lid was off. She let out a sigh and stepped forward, picking it up.

"I think someone's stealing," she said, her voice low as she looked back at Kathy. "This isn't a raccoon." She pointed at the can. "You know I donate as much as I can. I give extras to the church and people who need help. But sometimes food expires. It's not enough to give away, and I can't sell it, so I toss it." She paused. "Every day, for at least a week, the food I put in this can disappears. Sometimes the lid is off. Sometimes it's back on. But the food is always gone."

Kathy walked over, hands on her hips, inspecting the scene. "Yeah, okay ... but it's hard to tell anything back here. The gravel doesn't leave footprints. And there's nowhere to hide unless they're lightning fast."

"Not necessarily," Allison said. "If they know I go running with you and the back of the store is empty, they wouldn't have to hide. They'd just have to time it right." She turned toward her friend. "I'm going to talk to Ken. He usually knows if someone's fallen on hard times. If that's the case, I'll start putting together care packages. A loaf of bread doesn't cost me much. It wouldn't hurt my bottom line."

Kathy nodded immediately. "If you find out who it is, let me know. I'll do what I can to help, too."

Allison gave a quiet smile. "I'll do that. Come on in. I'll grab you a bottle of water."

"Thank you. The walk home relaxes me, but on days like this, a cold bottle of water sounds perfect."

Kathy followed her through the back door of the bakery, and as Allison reached into the fridge for two bottles of water, Kathy pointed toward the kitchen window. "Hey, is that somebody up front?"

Allison turned, squinting through the front of the shop. Her lips curled into a small smile. "Yeah. I think it's Seth …. and his partner."

Kathy's grin spread wide, and her eyes sparkled. "Seth Hansen?"

Allison nodded.

"And what do you mean by 'partner'? You never answered that."

"He has a dog," Allison said with a small laugh. "A *military working dog*. That's his partner. He was a dog handler in the military. The dog retired, and Seth went back to get him about a week ago."

Kathy raised her brows, thoroughly amused. "Let me guess. You're going to 'go see what he needs,' and I'm supposed to forget about this until tomorrow?"

Allison chuckled. "Yes. Let me handle this, and you go out the back. I'll see you tomorrow."

Kathy backed toward the rear exit, still smiling. "You'd better believe I want *all* the tea tomorrow. You're not dodging my questions."

"Get out of here." Allison laughed, giving her friend a playful push.

After Kathy waved and slipped out the back,

Allison walked through the bakery and unlocked the front door.

"Hey," she said, greeting him with a smile. "Did you need something?"

Seth looked between her and the sign in the window.

"I actually didn't realize it was past two. I've been letting Dad whittle out on the bench with Delbert. Trying to keep him on a routine, and the doctor said it would help." He gestured beside him. "This is Gomer, by the way."

The black German Shepherd sat neatly at his heel, poised and watchful.

Allison's heart softened immediately. She squatted down and extended her hand slowly. "Hey, big boy. How are you?"

The dog sniffed Allison's hand, gave a little huff, then licked her fingers with a single swipe of his tongue.

She smiled up at Seth. "He's gorgeous. May I pet him?"

"Sure," Seth said, watching with clear affection. "One of the things about Gomer is he's exceptionally friendly. Honestly, it was one of the reasons he was offered up for adoption. He's one of the best at search and rescue, and he can detect drugs in any room, but if someone offered him a belly scratch, he'd flop over and let them. Meanwhile, the person he was supposed to be tracking would just keep on running."

Allison laughed and ran her fingers through the thick fur at the dog's scruff. "You are absolutely gorgeous," she cooed to the dog, rubbing behind his ears. She offered her hand again. "Shake?"

Gomer lifted his paw and placed it gently in her palm.

"Oh, you're smart, too," she said, grinning and giving him another pat before standing. Her eyes returned to Seth. "Did you find out the results of your dad's tests?"

"The doc will call when she gets the rest of them in." His voice dropped, steady but subdued. "She thinks it's dementia. I keep wanting it to be mild, but everything the doctor said points to it being beyond that point." He exhaled slowly. "I'm trying to figure it all out as I go. That includes relearning when everything is open around here. I talked to your mom. She said it was no problem for Dad to sit out front and whittle as long as he wasn't being mean."

Allison smiled. "Chester whittled me a robin once. I still have it in my jewelry box. He told me my hair was as red as a robin's breast." She chuckled and touched the ends of her dark auburn hair. "Thank goodness it's gotten darker."

She paused and glanced at Seth, sympathy in her gaze. "He's a good man, Seth. I'm so sorry you're going through this. When he started getting mean, we knew someone needed to reach out to you or Sarah. He's always been curt, but it got worse there for a while."

"I heard," Seth said quietly, glancing toward the storefront. Then he turned back. "Do you think it'd be okay if I bought some bread for our dinner tonight?"

"Sure." She nodded. "Tell you what. Go around to the back. I'll grab something fresh for you. What do you need? Something for sandwiches or a baguette?"

"I'm making soup tonight. I was hoping for something Dad can slather with butter and dunk in it."

Allison laughed. "So, not a cracker kind of guy?"

"Never has been. Mom used to bake bread every week, right up until she passed. Dad loves his bread and butter."

Her expression softened. "I'm so sorry about your mom. I was out of town at my cousin's wedding in Colorado when the funeral happened. Did you come home for it?"

"Yeah. Me, Sarah, and her family. I couldn't stay long, though. Most of my emergency leave was used up traveling. First, getting back to the States, then out here with her."

"Where were you stationed?"

"I was working the MAJCOM program at Ramstein Air Force Base."

Allison's eyebrows lifted. "That sounds important. High-ranking or something?"

"Nope. Just pushing paper, not dogs. Hated every minute of it." He gave her a half-smile. "We'll go around back and meet you there."

As Seth and Gomer turned toward the side of the building, the dog stuck close to his leg, moving in perfect sync. There wasn't more than an inch of space between them.

Allison walked through the bakery, unlocked the back door, and called out, "You can come in. This is the mudroom. Past that is my break room. You both can wait there."

Seth glanced down at Gomer, then back at her. "Won't the county shut you down for letting a dog into the business?"

Allison laughed over her shoulder. "Not if she still wants her baguettes and strawberry rhubarb pies."

She disappeared into the front of the store and put together a small bag of dinner rolls he could warm up. After a moment's hesitation, she boxed up a blueberry pie and carried it back to the break room.

"Here you go," she said, handing him the bag.

Seth looked at it, eyebrows raised. "That's more than just bread."

She smiled. "You can call it a welcome home gift."

Their eyes met and lingered. Seth's expression shifted and softened. He smiled, one corner of his mouth tugging up before saying, "I'd better go grab Chester."

He stepped toward the door but paused, hand on the knob. "I'm glad you and Ken never got together."

Allison blinked, caught off guard. "Yeah? Why's that?"

He looked back at her with a slow, certain smile. "Because now I have a chance with the prettiest girl in school."

He opened the door and stepped outside. Allison stood frozen in place. Then she blinked again and reached up to touch her face. Totally felt it. Yep, not a dream. She shook her head and shut the door. Why did she all of the sudden feel like Alice spiraling down to Wonderland?

CHAPTER 7

*L*ater that evening, Seth reheated some chicken and rice soup he bought from the diner and brought it to the recliner on a tray. "Dinner," he said simply, setting the tray on the small table in front of Chester.

Chester blinked awake, eyes foggy with sleep. He took the tray without comment, then stared at the spoon as if it were something foreign in his hand.

Seth knelt down in front of him. "It's just soup, Pops. Chicken and rice."

"I can feed myself," Chester snapped, his voice low and rough. His hand trembled as he picked up the spoon.

Seth hesitated, then sat back on his heels. "Right. I'll be here if you need me."

Chester managed a few bites. Slow. Careful. After a moment, he set the spoon down with a quiet clink against the bowl. "Your mother used to make this kind of soup."

"I know."

Seth had watched her make it hundreds of times. He could make it in his sleep, but the diner's was easier and tasted good.

They sat in silence again. Not the brittle kind they used to fall into, full of resentment and unsaid words. This silence was softer. Heavier. Sadder.

And on Seth's end, it was more forgiving.

"Why'd you come back?" Chester asked suddenly, his voice quieter than before.

Seth looked at him. "Because you're my dad."

Chester gave a quiet grunt. He didn't say more. But he didn't need to.

As the sky outside the window turned gold with sunset and Gomer snored softly at Chester's feet, Seth sat beside his father and let the quiet hold them both.

He realized then that the strife between them might never be resolved. But maybe that wasn't the point anymore. Maybe now it was just about being here while there was still time left.

* * *

THE NEXT MORNING, Seth went out for a jog. He left Gomer in Chester's room with his father, figuring he'd exercise the dog later, after taking him to see the vet about his arthritis.

He wasn't gone long. Maybe thirty, thirty-five minutes, tops. But when he returned, the back door was wide open. Seth dropped the water bottle he'd been carrying, and it hit the porch with a dull thud.

His heart lurched. The kitchen was empty. Too quiet. The coffee pot sat cold and untouched. Chester's mug was already in the sink, and it was clean.

"Dad?" he called out as he moved quickly through the kitchen. "Gomer?"

No answer.

Seth jogged through the house, calling louder this time. He checked the bathroom, then the spare room. Nothing. He ran outside. The barn was empty. Panic prickled under his skin, hot and cold all at once. He grabbed his jacket from the hook by the door. The early fall air had bite, and if Chester had gone out without his coat…

Seth bolted. It took him nearly ten minutes to find them.

Chester was walking straight into the pasture a mile down the dirt road. He was in sock feet and flannel pajamas. Gomer padded beside him, the big shepherd sticking close but looking backward toward Seth and barking.

That was what led Seth to them. God knew it would've taken twice as long without Gomer's alert, loud and sharp in the morning quiet.

Chester had a bridle in one hand, his other swinging loosely at his side.

He kept calling out. "Dusty! Come on, boy! Dusty!"

Seth's chest tightened. Dusty had been gone for more than ten years. Seth approached carefully, not wanting to startle him.

"Pops?" he said softly. "Hey, what are you doing out here?"

Chester turned toward him, squinting against the sun. "Where the hell is the horse? I can't run the damn fence line without him."

Seth exhaled slowly, trying to keep his voice steady. "Dusty's gone, Pops. Remember? Besides, we're not riding today. Come on. Let's head back. We both need a cup of coffee."

Frowning, Chester looked down at the bridle in his hand like it had betrayed him.

"Somebody took him. I *know* it."

Seth stepped closer. "Nobody took him. He's been gone a long time." A beat passed. Then two.

And Chester's face crumpled. His anger dissolved, replaced by something lost and frightened. "I can't find the damn barn," he whispered. "Where's the barn, Seth?"

"It's okay. I got you, Pops."

Seth slid an arm gently around his father's shoulders and slowly turned him back toward the house. "Let's go home. I'll get you some coffee."

Chester muttered under his breath the entire way back. His tone was rough, disoriented, and agitated. Seth said nothing. He just listened. Each mumbled word was proof his father didn't understand where he was or what had just happened. When they stepped into the kitchen, Chester walked to the fridge, opened it, and tried to place the bridle inside.

Seth moved to stop him, reaching for the reins.

"I'm not stupid!" Chester shouted, jerking the leather out of his hands. "I know what I'm doing!"

Seth clamped his jaw shut, the muscles in his neck locked tight. God, he wanted to yell. Slam a door. Shout at the unfairness of it all. Shake something until the fear shook loose from his chest. But he didn't. He breathed. In. Out. Count to ten. Then, in the quietest voice he could manage, he said, "I know, Dad. I know. Let's sit down, all right?"

Eventually, Chester did. He dropped into his recliner with a weight that seemed to deflate him completely. His hands shook. His breath came shallow. His eyes stared past the window, vacant and unfocused.

Something had been taken from Chester that morning, and Seth felt like he was standing in the rubble of that violence, powerless to rebuild it.

He brought a cup of coffee and handed it to Chester, who stared at it for a long moment before taking a sip. When he looked up, his eyes were glassy, glistening with tears. "I think something's wrong with me, Seth," he whispered.

Seth sat down across from him, his voice soft, steady. "Yeah, Pops. I know. But you're not alone. You'll never be alone again. I'm here. I got you."

JUST PAST SUNSET, Seth sat at the kitchen table surrounded by a small mountain of paperwork. There were bills, brochures, pamphlets with resources for caregivers, options for memory care ...

All of it heavier than stone. He rubbed the back

of his neck, blinking through the weight of decision fatigue, when he heard the soft shuffle of sock-covered feet in the hallway.

Chester appeared in the doorway wearing plaid pajama pants and a faded old T-shirt that read *Property of the U.S. Army, 1964.*

Seth had no idea where the shirt had come from. Chester was never in the Army. And definitely not in 1964.

"Are you making popcorn?" Chester asked.

Seth blinked. "No, but I could."

Chester sniffed the air. "I smell it. I smell popcorn."

Seth laughed under his breath. "You smell the dog's feet. I just put ointment on one. Gomer ripped a gash between his paw pads while he was out in the field with you today."

Chester squinted at Gomer, who was stretched out nearby.

"Well, I'll be damned," he muttered. "Damn dog smells like popcorn. And you know what? That dog likes me."

Seth smiled, his chest warming. "He sure does, Pops."

And Seth was sure of that fact. Gomer had not left Chester's side since they'd returned home that morning. The old shepherd had chosen his next duty.

Chester.

Seth laughed, really laughed, for the first time in days. "You want me to make some popcorn anyway?"

Chester shrugged and wandered into the kitchen. He opened the cabinet like it was routine, like nothing at all had happened that morning. "If we're eating dog feet, we might as well put butter on them."

Seth grabbed a bag from the shelf and tossed it into the microwave. "I'll take mine with extra toenails."

Chester cracked a smile and lowered into the chair across from him. "You always were a weird kid."

"And you were the one who let me build a catapult in the backyard."

"Hell of a shot, though," Chester said. "You launched your cousin's bike clean over the chicken coop." They both chuckled, the sound soft and full of memory. And for a brief moment, the fog seemed to lift from Chester's face. His eyes were sharp. His smile was real, not tight or confused, but natural. Alive.

"I miss your mama," Chester said after a quiet

pause. "She always burned the popcorn, but she made it anyway."

Seth nodded, his voice quiet. "I miss her, too."

The microwave dinged. He stood and poured the popcorn into a bowl, adding extra butter just the way his dad liked it. Carrying it back to the table, he set it down between them and took a seat across from Chester.

They passed the bowl back and forth in silence, each man reaching in, eating, and chewing with no conversation necessary. Just two souls who had once been oceans apart settling into the rhythm of something that felt like old times.

Eventually, Chester leaned back in his chair with a satisfied sigh. "You gonna tell the neighbors I lost a horse that's been dead for a decade?"

Seth grinned. "Only if you tell them I cried during *Field of Dreams* when we watched it last night."

Chester snorted, then shook his head. "That part where the dad shows up? Gets me every damn time."

Seth's smile softened, his eyes meeting his father's. "Yeah, me, too, Pops."

For that one night, the diagnosis didn't matter. The wandering, the fear, hell, even the doctors' appointments ... all of it faded to the background.

They just were. A father and a son, passing a bowl of buttery popcorn and sharing the kind of quiet that only came from love that had weathered distance, time, and pain. Just a moment of peace before the storm returned.

CHAPTER 8

*A*llison wouldn't lie to herself. Her heart beat just a little faster, and a smile tugged at the corners of her mouth when she saw Seth and Chester pull up in front of the general store.

For the last week, they'd had a routine. Seth brought his father into town around one each afternoon. Chester would sit on the bench with Delbert, carving and talking, while Seth lingered just long enough to make sure he was okay. Gomer parked himself beside Chester like a silent sentry.

Then Seth would head down the street and slip through the alley to her back door.

They'd visit. He always left by two, so she could close up and go for her daily run, but those forty-five minutes? They'd become something she quietly cherished.

There were no expectations with Seth. He didn't know much about her past, at least, not the parts that haunted her. Those haunting insecurities that had caused her to act out weren't a memory for him. He hadn't seen the push and pull of her controlling grip over Ken. He hadn't witnessed her being a bitch to him. He was a fresh canvas, a breath of fresh air, and with him, she could just be the Allison she'd fought hard to grow into. Did she still slip into the insecurities? Sure, every now and then, but she had a way to climb out of that spiral and stop the need to control events and people.

In those quiet minutes on her wooden back steps, sipping iced tea in the shade, laughing at his jokes or stories about dogs he'd handled, she felt something she hadn't realized she'd missed until now. Peace. She smiled and stared at him as he spoke. Emotions were forming for her. Emotions that drew her to this man in a way she'd never experienced before. Her heart tripped when she saw him, and she smiled at the thought. It didn't scare her to open herself up to him, and that feeling was freeing.

She'd started doing her closing chores earlier, just to make sure she had time for him. Even Edna

Michaelson had come in early for her order, which was unusual, but she didn't mind.

Today, she'd thrown out only a very small amount of food. Most of the sweets had been picked up by the church for Sunday service. The leftovers were still good, but per state rules, she either had to give them away or discard them before the expiration date.

Allison leaned against the front wall of her shop. Her chores were done, her till counted out and prepped for the morning.

She smiled as she watched Seth stand up. The big shepherd stayed curled at Chester's feet as the older man whittled with Delbert. Chester's hand gently patted the dog's head now and then. A sensation of warmth and happiness washed over her. She wrapped her arms around herself and laughed freely. She was falling for that man. Too quick? Probably, but that was a worry for another time. Seth turned and headed toward the alley, just like he always did. Allison flipped the lock on the front door and hurried toward the back, her smile still lingering.

She opened the door and stopped in her tracks.

A girl, or maybe a young woman, stood at the trash can, holding the lid and digging through the contents.

Allison's hand went to her chest.

"Excuse me," she said, her voice sharp with surprise. "Can I help you?"

The woman jerked back, eyes wide. She dropped the lid and ran.

Just then, Seth rounded the corner. "Who was that?" Seth asked, stepping up beside her.

Allison shook her head. "I don't know. I've never seen her before."

"She didn't look too good, did she?"

"No. She looked ... dirty. Skinny. Really skinny. I should call Ken."

"Where did she go?" Seth frowned and walked around the building. When he returned, he shook his head. "She's gone. Not visible from anywhere. A regular Houdini."

"She's the one who's been taking food from my trash," Allison said, hands on her hips.

"What are you talking about?"

"For the past week, maybe more, I've noticed food disappearing. Only the bags with expired stuff. Nothing else touched. I don't overbake, so it's not much, but it's always gone."

Seth's frown deepened. "You think she's been living off what you're throwing away?"

"I hope not," Allison said, voice tight. "It's not

enough to keep a bird alive. Maybe I should start leaving a sandwich or something more."

Seth crossed his arms over his chest. "This is a small town. I'm surprised no one's seen her."

"I haven't been to the diner lately," Allison admitted. "I've been swamped with prebaking for the Fall Festival. But that's where the gossip lives."

"Maybe we should head over," Seth said. "You can keep an eye on the store from there, and Chester's fine with Delbert. I'll buy you a cup of coffee."

Allison hesitated. "Edna's probably still over there. If we walk in together, they're going to say we're dating." An electric feeling zipped through her when he smiled and winked at her.

"That wouldn't bother me in the slightest." He grinned. "Which reminds me. Can I get your number? You know, for a text. Or a phone call."

Allison stared at him, brows raised. Yep, emotions, all kinds of emotions, were doing the ping-pong-ping through her brain. "Are you serious?"

"Of course, I'm serious. I asked, didn't I?"

She pulled her phone from her pocket, and her hands shook a little. "All right. Give me your number."

He rattled it off, and she punched it in, sending a

quick text to confirm. "Thank you." When his eyes dropped to her lips, she about fainted. Flat-out falling on her face type of fainting. A truck trundled down the street, breaking her from her trance. "Oh, wait. I need to lock the back door, and I've got something for you." She sprinted back up the steps and into the break room.

Allison grabbed the lavender box, filled with little things she thought Seth, Chester, and especially Gomer might enjoy.

To be honest, most of it was for Gomer. Homemade, bone-shaped treats with dog-safe ingredients like sweet potatoes and blueberries. She'd never made dog biscuits before, but she hoped they turned out okay.

She came back out, locking the door behind her, and handed the box to Seth.

"What's all this?"

"Something for you, Chester, and Gomer. Gomer gets the bone-shaped ones. Don't eat them," she said with a smirk. "I mean ... You could. But they're not going to taste as good as the stuff I made for you two."

Seth peeked into the box and chuckled. "You're going to spoil us."

"You know," she said as they started walking, "as

hard as you're working with your dad, a little spoiling wouldn't hurt."

"Let's go to the diner," Seth said, tucking the box under his arm, placing his hand on her back. "I'll take this back to the store later. No sense in confusing Chester right now."

They crossed the street diagonally, waving at Phil and his nephew-in-law, Alex Thompson, who both owned and worked the repair shop and gas station.

The bell over the diner door chimed as they stepped inside. Every head turned in their direction. Ken and Samantha were sitting in the booth immediately inside the door. It was Ken's usual booth, due to the easy exit if he had to respond to something. Seth stopped and shook Ken's hand, and then Ken introduced his wife.

"Ma'am," Seth said after greeting her, "I'd like to schedule an appointment with you. Chester and I need to get his business in order."

Samantha extended her hand, and Seth took it. Allison faded back a bit. No matter how kind Sam was and how many times Ken had forgiven her, being with both of them was an uncomfortable situation for her. It was *her* issue, not theirs.

"So nice to meet you, Seth. I have time next week, unless it's something urgent?" She glanced across the street to where Chester, Delbert, and Gomer sat in the shade.

"No, ma'am. Next week is fine," Seth assured her.

"Then how about Wednesday, about eleven?"

Seth glanced toward the window and nodded to his dad. "Would it be possible to make it closer to this time? I'm trying to keep him on a schedule. It seems to help."

Sam nodded immediately. "Sure. One?"

"Perfect. Thank you for making time for us." Seth smiled back at her. "And congratulations."

"Thank you so much, we're so excited, and it isn't a problem at all." Sam looked around him and smiled at her. "Allison, the pie you sent as congratulations was delicious. I don't know how you make such flakey crust."

Allison smiled. "Practice. Years and years of practice."

"Well, it paid off," Sam said and raised her coffee cup to Allison. "You've mastered the art."

"Thank you, but we came over here to find some information. Since you're here, I should probably tell you we may have an issue." She stepped forward a bit and lowered her voice. "There was a girl, maybe a young woman, today who was digging in my trash can. I think she's been taking some of the expired products from the trash can to eat."

Ken straightened and looked around. "Sit down for a moment, will you?" Seth slid into the seat across from Ken and Sam, placing the box alongside the window. He glanced over to check in on his dad as Allison sat down, too. Her leg touched his, and the feel of his hard muscles sent a little tingle of excitement through her, but Ken rerouted her thoughts with his question, "What are you talking about?"

Allison blinked and then leaned forward, lowering her voice, "For the last week, maybe a little longer, something has been getting into my garbage cans. The thing is, nothing is disturbed except the food I have to throw out because I can't sell it or give it away. Today I saw a girl at the trash can. She was bruised and so damn thin. Seth saw her, too."

Seth nodded and carried on in the same quiet tone, "Briefly. Brunette, five feet six or seven, bruises on her face, the side of her neck, and down one arm. They were about two weeks old, with a yellowing and fading appearance. She was wearing white tennis shoes, blue jeans, and a white or gray shirt."

Allison blinked and turned to look at him. He glanced at her. "I saw her longer than you did,"

Allison said. "And I couldn't have told him half that information. How did you see all of that?"

"I was a cop for my entire career in the Air Force. MWD handlers are security personnel, and we primarily work on law enforcement issues unless we're forward deployed for base security."

Allison couldn't help but notice the way his arm flexed. Her eyes dipped to his bicep and then back to his eyes. He winked at her. Mortified, she snapped her head in Ken's direction and immediately changed the subject. "She looked way too skinny. Has there been any reports of a runaway or anything?"

Ken frowned and shook his head. "No, nothing. I can go back and look at other counties. Do you think she's that young?"

"I don't know." She looked at Seth. "Maybe twenty at the oldest?"

"Honestly, I'm crap at ages. She could be anywhere from sixteen to twenty-five." He shrugged. "Sorry about that."

"No, what you've given me is enough. I'll let the deputies know to be on the lookout for her. Strange she hasn't asked for help or anything." Ken looked out the window. "We've had a couple of strangers in town lately, but they've moved on."

Seth leaned a bit closer. "You think she may have gotten free from an abusive situation?"

Sam nodded. "That's exactly what I'm thinking."

"I'm going to leave her a decent meal tomorrow and a note letting her know she can trust me."

"That could be a hard sell, but it couldn't hurt," Sam said. "Most people on the run from abusive situations fear everything and everyone. They have no reason to trust."

Allison sighed; her gut dropped. "I have to try."

"Please do," Ken said before turning to Sam. "Babe, I'm going to head back to the office and start working on this. I'll put the description out to see if anyone's been reported missing locally. If we can't find anything, I'll push it out to the state and nationally. If we can get her to trust us and get her story, that would help."

"I'm done, too," Sam said. "I'll leave with you. Seth, it was a pleasure meeting you, and I look forward to talking with you and your dad." Ken stood up, helped Sam out of the booth, and dropped money for their lunch. "Tell Corrie the meal was great."

"I heard you, and thank you," Corrie said as she approached the table. "Sorry, I was prepping breakfast for tomorrow and didn't hear you come inside. What can I get you?"

"Nothing for me," Allison said and glanced at the clock on the wall. "Kathy and I are running in twenty minutes. If I eat anything now, I'll be in misery."

"For you?" Corrie looked at Seth. "Sorry, do I know you?"

"I don't think so, ma'am. I'm Seth Hansen. Chester is my father. I understand he's been asked not to come here any longer."

The woman's face fell. "I hated doing that. Chester was just so out of control. We have our other customers to consider. If you've got his temper under control, he's welcome back."

"I understand," Seth said, smiling. "He won't be spending much time in town anyway."

Allison nudged him. "Did you want a coffee or something?"

"No, I'm good. Glad we got to talk to Ken," Seth said.

"Then I'll leave you two to visit." Corrie took the dirty dishes in a stack that rivaled the Leaning Tower of Pisa.

Allison slid out of the bench and glanced over at Edna Michaelson. The woman had a smile the

Cheshire Cat would have been jealous of. Allison knew better than to walk out without introducing Seth and setting the record straight. They were not dating. Although she wouldn't mind ... No, she wouldn't start wishing for things that weren't going to happen.

Touching Seth's elbow, she tilted her head to the side. He glanced at the table she was indicating and smiled. "The hen party still owns the back corner booth, huh?"

"Some things never change." Allison laughed as they made their way to her booth.

"Edna, do you remember Seth Hansen?" Allison asked, gesturing to him.

"Miss Edna," Seth said, balancing the box in one hand and offering the other. "It's a pleasure to see you again."

Edna took his hand and beamed. "Of course, I remember you, Seth. How nice of you to come back and take care of your daddy. We've all been very, very worried about him."

Seth smiled, polite and measured. But Allison noticed his eyes didn't quite match the smile.

"Thank you," he said softly, then stood straighter, holding his lavender box.

"I see Allison has hooked you up with all the

goodies." Edna's voice left no doubt that she *wasn't* talking about the baked goods. Allison glared at her, but the woman dared to smile wider.

Seth chuckled, obviously noting the exchange. "Dog biscuits for Gomer, my retired military working dog, and a few goodies for Chester and me." He turned to the other ladies at the booth. "Miss Belinda, Miss Doris, it's good to see you looking so well," he added with a nod. "If you'll excuse me, it's time to collect Chester and make sure Delbert gets home."

"I'll go with you." She wasn't staying for the Edna Inquisition. They said their farewells, and Allison walked out with him. "I'm so sorry for that, but if we didn't stop by to say hi to her, the woman would have us married by next week."

Seth chuckled. "Not much changes in a small town."

Allison glanced across the street at the two men sitting on the bench. "How's Delbert doing? Your dad used to take care of him."

"As far as I can tell, he's still getting along. I made my father a promise that when he was no longer able to take care of him, I would."

"Delbert isn't any trouble. Just slow," Allison said as she walked Seth back to his truck.

"He used to be very smart, or so my dad has told me. He was kicked in the head by a bull when he was a teenager. My family has cared for him for as long as I can remember. Delbert had a small cottage on my grandpa's place. When he and Grandma passed, Delbert became Dad's responsibility."

"You know Mr. Hollister pays for his groceries, and Mr. Marshall lets him stay rent-free in one of his little cabins," Allison said as they slowed to a stroll, neither one seeming to want to end the talk today.

"Both the Hollisters and Marshalls are good people. They take care of this little town." Seth looked around. "But it has grown. At least doubled in size since I left."

"We're kind of proud of the community it's become," Allison agreed as she looked up and down the main street, where she saw Kathy jogging down the road. "There's my running partner."

Seth opened his truck door and put the box on the seat. "Is it okay if I call later?" Seth was turned so Chester could only see his back.

She smiled up at him. "I'd like that, but I want to warn you, I might get the idea you like me if you keep this up."

"I've always liked you, Allison." He winked at her

and nodded down the road before he turned and walked up the wooden steps to the front of her parents' store. "You'd better get going, or you're going to be late."

She stood there like an idiot watching him walk up the steps before her brain engaged, and she spun, setting out at a quick jog to intercept Kathy. They fell into step, and Kathy smiled as they passed the store. Both Chester and Seth waved at them. Allison had to give Kathy credit; she waited until they were out of earshot before asking, "So, do you have any tea for me?"

Allison laughed. "Man, do I ever."

CHAPTER 9

Seth stared down at his phone, where Allison's name and number were glowing on the screen. It had been a couple of days since she'd given him her number. He hesitated for a breath, then tapped the call button as he stepped onto the front porch. The evening air was crisp, cool enough that he considered grabbing a jacket, but the cold didn't bother him much. Gomer wandered the perimeter of the yard, nose to the ground, sniffing his way along the fence line with quiet purpose.

The phone rang three times before she picked up. "Hey," she said, her voice warm. "How are you doing?"

He could hear a television murmuring in the background. "Did I interrupt anything?"

"No," Allison said. "Just watching an old movie. I usually head to bed early, so this is my wind-down time."

"I figured you'd be up at the crack of dawn to start baking."

"Well, I'm lucky I live above the bakery," she replied with a soft chuckle. "So, my commute isn't exactly long. I'm usually at work by four thirty."

Seth let out a mock groan. "Now I feel lazy. I'm not up until five thirty or six."

"Yes, I would absolutely call you a slacker," Allison teased. "But you've got a lot more stress than I do. My business kind of runs on autopilot these days. I've got regulars with regular orders, and I've figured out what sells and what doesn't. It's a rhythm now."

"I'm impressed by your business acumen," Seth said. "I don't think I could run a business. I hate paperwork, which is why I retired after twenty-two instead of staying longer. And it's a good thing I did, with Dad's decline and all."

"Have you gotten the results yet?" He knew exactly what results she was referring to. They'd talked about it a couple of times, how the wait for the results was hard on both him and Chester. "I got the call this afternoon. We go to Belle Fourche tomorrow," he said. "The doctor's got the final assessments in."

"That's going to be a stressful day for both of you," Allison said, her voice quieter. "I wish I could do something to make it easier for you."

"There's nothing to do," Seth replied. "Just talking to you helps. Sometimes I have the same conversation with Dad all day."

"Well," she said, her voice brightening, "I promise our conversations will always be varied."

The corner of his mouth ticked up. "And I thank you for that." He paused for a moment, then added, "I was wondering if you wouldn't mind having dinner with me one day next week. It would have to be here, and I'd cook."

"Or," she offered, "I can bring dinner out to you and your dad. And, of course, something for Gomer."

Seth laughed softly. "But that would be *you* providing the date, not *me*. And I'm not sure how I feel about that."

Allison's voice lowered, almost angry, "You're not one of those macho men who has to be in charge of the date, are you?"

He blinked, then shook his head. "I never really thought of it that way, but yeah, I guess that *was* what I was thinking. Is that outdated?"

Allison laughed, a warm, easy sound. "No, I was just yanking your leg. Honestly, it'd be easier for me to cook and bring it out. Maybe one day, we'll get to go *out* on a real date, and you can buy me some fancy food in a sit-down restaurant. But for now, let's take the easy route. I know how to bake a thing or two, and I've been told my cooking's not bad either."

"If your cooking is as good as your baking, I have no doubt I'll enjoy every morsel. You sure you don't mind?"

"Not at all. What do you say about next Saturday?"

"That's perfect," Seth said. "I've started cleaning the house, but it's a lot of work. Chester's not exactly a hoarder, but he's kept a *lot* of stuff over the years that probably should've been thrown out a long time ago. I've been working through it slowly. As long as he doesn't get too agitated, I move the stuff to the back porch. From there, it goes into the fire pit or the dump."

"He's been alone for a while," Allison said. "I couldn't see your mom letting him collect all that stuff."

"Oh, heck no," Seth replied with a quiet laugh. "My mom was hell on wheels and kept Chester in line. She took care of him, and in return, he worked his butt off to give her the things he thought she wanted. They had a good relationship. She understood him in a way I never could. Although," he added with a dry chuckle, "Mom used to say Chester and I were hit over the head with the same stick. Both stubborn. Both prideful. Both thinking we knew too much for our own good."

Allison went quiet for a moment. "I don't know what I'll do when my parents pass," she said softly. "Not that they have any health issues, thank God, but I think it's going to carve out a hole in my soul."

Seth made a low sound of agreement. "You never really stop thinking about them," he murmured. "Mom's been gone for a long time now, and still, there are days when I think, I should show her this, or I wish I could talk to her about that." He exhaled. "But this is turning into a depressing talk, and I didn't mean to do that."

"I'm so sorry," Allison said quickly. "I didn't mean to lead you down that path."

"You didn't lead me anywhere," Seth said, surprised by her apology. "It's not your fault. That's just where the conversation went." He paused for a moment. "You do that a lot, you know."

Allison was quiet for a moment before asking, "Do what a lot?"

"You take the blame. Or put yourself down." Seth's voice was low but sure. "You don't seem to realize that you're beautiful. That I'm attracted to you. I saw the disbelief on your face when I told you I thought you were the cutest girl in school. But you were. To me. You were also too young for me to approach back then, and oh, by the way, Ken was always hanging around."

Allison snorted softly. "Yeah, well, that relationship went down in Hollister history as the worst one ever."

"I'm sure there are worse," Seth said. "And I'm sure there are relationships you don't even know about. But you really do need to let that go. Ken doesn't hold any ill will. And when we talked to Sam today, she didn't seem to have a problem with you either. Though you were *very* quiet for a while."

"Observant of you," Allison said, a little laugh in her voice.

"It's the law enforcement training," Seth replied. "Tend to notice things like that." He let the pause stretch just long enough before asking, "Why haven't you forgiven yourself?"

Allison let out a breath, this time slower. "You know, I'm not sure. I still can't say exactly why I won't let myself find forgiveness. I know Ken's forgiven me. I know Sam is a sweetheart and holds no grudge. But something in me still believes I deserve the punishment. Does that make sense?"

"What are you talking about?"

"Well, you know Ken and I dated in high school, right?"

"Yep."

"I was a bitch to him. I mean, when we first started going out in high school, it was fun. Having a date for the dances, someone to hang out with in the halls, having a guy around in the summer when we went to the lake or such."

"Yeah, typical high school stuff. What's bitchy about that?"

"Nothing. It was after that. See, when I was growing up, I was traumatized by some people who picked on me. It built this ... well, a vortex of insecurities inside me. I knew Ken liked me, even if I didn't return the affection. I used it to control him, to keep him close, to make myself feel better." She paused for a moment. "I've worked through all of that, and I've made amends, but as I said, I still feel bad about it and think they shouldn't forgive me. I hope that doesn't make me less in your eyes."

"Not in the slightest," Seth said honestly. "I don't think you need to worry about it. They seem cool with you, but if that's how you feel, it's real for you."

Allison laughed again, softer this time. "Oh my God. You sound just like Dr. Wheeler."

Seth chuckled. "I think I need to meet this guy. Sounds like my kind of people."

"He totally is," she said. "He used to work at a maximum security prison. A serial killer actually tracked him down here in Hollister."

Seth sat up straighter. "Say what now?" He leaned forward, elbows on his knees. "Repeat that."

"Oh, it's a long story," Allison said, amused. "But yeah. A serial killer found him. From what I understand, they had a history. It happened during that massive tornado a few years back that took out a lot of the old buildings here in town. It was chaos. And Jeremiah, that's Dr. Wheeler, ended up going one-on-one with the killer. Needless to say, I'm skipping over a *lot* of details, but everything worked out. Jeremiah decided to stay, put down roots. He's married now, has kids, and he primarily works for the Marshalls."

Seth frowned. "The Marshalls? Oh, you mean…"

"Yeah," Allison confirmed, her tone quiet. "We don't talk about it. We don't confirm it. But we all know it's there. It's the best kept non-secret in

Hollister. And if a stranger ever asks you about it?" She paused, voice a shade lower. "You know nothing. That's the way it works, and that's the way we keep it going," Allison said, her voice quieting with tiredness.

"So I've been told. Ken made all that pretty clear the first time he talked to me." Seth heard her yawn and smiled. "I'm gonna let you get to bed. I know it's late."

"Not for normal people." She laughed. "I can talk." She yawned again.

"You *could*," Seth said gently, "or you could fall asleep and wake up refreshed in the morning."

There was a pause and a small laugh from her side of the connection. "True."

"Thanks for talking to me, Allison."

"You can call me anytime, Seth, not just when you need someone who won't say the same thing fifteen times in a row. I really do enjoy your company. I enjoy our talks … and I enjoy being around you."

Seth's smile widened, his heart softening at her words. "And I do think you were the cutest girl in school," he said. "And I enjoy talking with you, too."

Allison chuckled, but her voice held a hint of vulnerability. "Seth Hansen, I keep telling you, if you keep saying things like that, I'm going to start to think you like me."

"You've said that before, and you should believe it," he said. "Because I do." A quiet beat passed between them before he quietly added, "Goodnight, Allison."

"Seth?"

"Yeah?"

"I really like you."

"I really like you, too." He chuckled and then drew a long breath. "I'm not good at the small talk, Allison. I never have been. I guess I get that from Chester, but when we're together, it's good. I mean, you're so fucking sexy, I could devour you."

Her gasp was audible. "What?"

"I know you said you were insecure. You don't need to feel that way with me. Woman, you light every fire I have. I know that probably isn't the most romantic thing to say, but it's the truth. On top of that, you're fun and easy to be with. I don't have to work at it, you know? You are easy in the best possible way."

"Seth Hansen, did you just call me easy? Twice?"

He laughed at her mock outrage. "Maybe, but I meant it in a good way."

She laughed and then quieted. "I really like you,

Seth. You light my fires, too, and for you, I'll be easy." She paused and then laughed, adding, "To be around."

"Get some sleep, woman. Lord knows we both need it."

"All right. Call me if you need me. I will always answer."

He smiled. "I will. Good night."

"Good night."

* * *

ALLISON SET her cell phone on the small table near the couch and clicked off the television. The soft glow from the screen faded, leaving the living room dim and quiet. She smiled in the darkness and closed her eyes. Flirting with Seth sent a rush of energy through her, and she wished he were on the couch with her now. She wanted to feel the warmth of his big body against her. That tingling sensation whenever he was around ghosted through her, and she could smell his cologne. His deep rumbling voice on the phone had set her body on fire. What could he do to her with his hands? His lips? A full-body shiver ran through her, and her core ached in a way she'd never imagined possible from a phone call. My God, the man was amazing, and she prayed she didn't screw it up. Open, honest, and no secrets. She nodded to herself. If this relationship didn't work out, it wouldn't be because she didn't express her emotions correctly.

She glanced at the clock on the wall. It was nearing nine.

With a sigh, she walked into the kitchen, her footsteps echoing softly against the old wooden floorboards that creaked with familiar comfort. She moved with purpose, opening the fridge and pulling out what she needed.

A large turkey sandwich, stacked high and wrapped in wax paper, went into an insulated bag. She added two bottles of water, a small take-out container of salad from the diner, and then paused.

Pulling a clean sheet from her to-do list pad, she flipped it over and wrote on the back in neat, looping script:

I think you need this. I won't hurt you. I live above the bakery. If you need help, come to me. I promise the people of this town are safe.

She signed her name and tucked the note into the bag. On impulse, she added a couple of packets of ibuprofen, a small pouch of hand wipes, and the candy bar she'd been trying to resist all week. It was chocolate with almonds, which was her favorite.

She sealed the bag, then made her way down the narrow staircase to the rear entrance of the bakery. The quiet of Hollister at night always felt different than the day. There was no traffic, no farm trucks rumbling by, or teenagers hanging out by the gas station after school. Just the occasional gust of wind sweeping across the prairie, carrying the scent of hayfields and pine.

She lifted the garbage can lid and slipped the insulated bag into the clear liner she'd already placed inside. She carefully closed the lid and glanced around, letting her eyes adjust to the dark.

The alley behind the bakery was barely lit, with only a single overhead bulb glowing near the back door. The edges of the building cast long, soft shadows onto gravel, and beyond that, the wide openness of rural South Dakota stretched toward a star-splashed sky.

"If you can hear me," she said softly into the darkness, "there's no need to be afraid. If you're in trouble, we can help."

She rubbed her arms against the chill, the night breeze pressing against her skin. She'd pull out an old coat tomorrow and leave it in the clean liner if the woman didn't approach her by then. Nights were getting chilly as October was fast approaching. Allison waited a bit. But no shadow moved, no figure stepped forward from the gloom. Allison stood for a few more moments, listening. With a quiet sigh, she walked back upstairs, her hand sliding automatically into the pocket of her hoodie to check for her keys. She turned the lock behind her, not because she was afraid, not in Hollister. But because, when she'd first moved out of her parents' house, her father had made her promise always to lock the door at night.

She smiled at the memory. Every so often, her dad would stop by just to make sure she had. He never asked, just tugged on the knob with satisfaction and nodded when it didn't budge.

Even now, she was still their baby. The only child of a close-knit family, she understood their concern. Her parents could be protective, but they'd always given her space to grow and build her own life. Only two things were mandatory. She needed to lock the door and come home for Sunday dinner.

She ensured the house was tidy and all appliances were off before flipping off the lights. Out of curiosity, she went to the window and gently pulled back the curtain. Outside, the can sat still beneath the weak glow of the alley light.

The lid was off. Allison smiled sadly. She prayed the woman had heard her words, and, hopefully, whoever she was, would realize she was safe there and that she wasn't alone anymore.

No, the woman in the alley wasn't alone anymore, and neither was she. She had Seth now, didn't she?

CHAPTER 10

The waiting room was quiet. Only the faint rustle of magazines and the soft hum of the HVAC system filled the space. Seth sat stiffly, one leg bouncing with his hands clasped tightly between his knees. Across from him, Chester stared at the television mounted in the corner. The volume was off, but news headlines scrolled across the screen, something about congressional hearings.

"Mr. Hansen?" a nurse called out cheerfully. Seth stood, automatically reaching for his father's elbow. Chester swatted his hand away but stood without complaint. They followed the nurse down a long hallway that smelled faintly of antiseptic. As they passed rooms filled with murmured conversations and sharp fluorescent lights, Seth felt his jaw tighten.

Dr. Carlisle, the same physician from the previous visit, greeted them with a nod and a soft smile. "Please, sit down," she said, motioning toward the chairs across from her desk.

Seth and Chester did as she asked, and when they were settled, she said, "I've reviewed the scans and lab results." Dr. Carlisle continued, getting straight to the point, "The imaging confirms what we suspected. There is entropy in the temporal and parietal lobes, consistent with Alzheimer's disease. Your vitamin levels and thyroid levels are normal. There is no sign of a stroke or tumor, which is good news. You do have a UTI that we'll take care of with some antibiotics."

Seth sat up straighter. Somewhere in that brief explanation, tucked neatly between the tests and the reassurances, she'd confirmed it. His father had Alzheimer's.

His gut dropped to the floor, and he could feel his hopes dying. He licked his dry lips and asked, "So … it's official, then?"

Dr. Carlisle met his gaze without flinching. "Yes. The diagnosis is early to moderate Alzheimer's."

She glanced at Chester. Seth did, too. His father looked from the doctor to his son, his expression unreadable.

Seth leaned forward slightly. "So, what's next?"

"I've started the paperwork for the Alzheimer's registry," Dr. Carlisle replied. "There are medication options. We can try donepezil and memantine. They won't stop the disease, but they may help alleviate symptoms and delay the progression."

Seth turned to look at his dad, who sat stiffly, staring at the doctor like she might be setting him up for a joke.

"What about side effects?" Seth asked.

"Mostly nausea, some dizziness," she said. "But most patients tolerate the medication well. We'll start at a low dose and monitor how he responds."

Then she turned to Chester. "Chester, how are you feeling today?" Chester blinked, as if realizing for the first time that he was still part of the conversation. "I feel fine," he said roughly. "I just forget stuff sometimes. That's normal for my age."

His voice had shifted. Defensive now. Dr. Carlisle's smile was kind, patient. "Chester, some forgetfulness *is* normal. However, what we're seeing in your scans and tests is more than that. That's why it's important we take action now. The medication can help you."

Chester frowned. "I don't need or want pills." His father stiffened. Seth could see it happening. The line had been drawn, and his father's heels were already digging in. When Chester decided to become pigheaded, nothing would stop him. Seth wasn't about to give him the chance.

He leaned in, his voice quiet. "Pops. This isn't about needing them. It's about making things easier. For both of us."

The doctor nodded. "And it gives you more good time to spend with your son," she added. That seemed to reach Chester. He looked down at his hands, shoulders still tense, but he gave a grudging nod.

"We'll also connect you with a social worker and a care coordinator," Dr. Carlisle said to Seth. "You don't have to figure this out alone."

Seth felt a lump rise in his throat. Maybe he didn't *have* to do it alone, but he sure as hell *felt* like the weight of the world was sitting on his shoulders. The doctor told them she'd called in a prescription to the hospital pharmacy for pickup and talked about follow-ups before she stood.

"Thank you," Seth said, voice hoarse as he reached to shake her hand. Dr. Carlisle returned the handshake and stood.

As they turned to leave, Chester glanced around the room with unfocused eyes, like he'd forgotten where he was. Seth gently placed a hand on his elbow. This time, Chester didn't swat him away. He let him help.

* * *

THREE DAYS HAD PASSED since they'd returned from Belle Fourche. The pill organizer sat on the kitchen counter like a small, quiet sentinel and a silent promise. But Seth wasn't convinced that the promise could be kept.

Every morning's square held the same tiny white tablet: donepezil. It looked harmless. The doctor had said it might help Chester hold onto pieces of himself a little longer. That was worth trying.

"All right, Pops," Seth said, balancing the pills between two fingers as he approached the recliner. "Time to take your medication."

Chester looked up from a crossword puzzle he hadn't been able to finish all week. It used to take him an hour, max. "Already? Didn't I just take that?"

"No, sir. It's morning. Breakfast, meds, then your walk."

Chester studied him for a beat too long before taking the pill. He dry-swallowed it with a grimace. "Tastes like a stick of chalk."

"Ever eaten one of those?" Seth asked.

Chester narrowed his eyes at him. "Yes, on a dare, and it tasted better than that pill."

Seth chuckled and returned to the kitchen to rinse out his father's coffee mug, thinking grimly that chalky pills were still better than watching him slip further and further away. So, they built a routine. Wake. Eat. Meds. A short walk down the gravel lane. Then, there were puzzles or music, lunch, and a drive into town, so Chester could sit and whittle with Delbert while Seth ran errands or talked with Allison.

The structure helped. Chester, for the most part, knew what they were doing and when. The occasional slips were hard on both of them. The routine worked and anchored their days.

But it didn't stop the damn disease. Sometimes Chester forgot he'd already eaten and asked for lunch again. Sometimes he lost words mid-sentence, frustration taking over until he gave up talking altogether.

Seth had taped reminders all over the fridge. *Things to Do*, *Things to Watch*, and *Things to Talk to the Doctor About.*

He set alarms on his phone for everything: pills, water, check-ins. He found out that his father would forget to drink water, which was probably what had led to his UTI. The UTIs could cause his father to become combative, and Dr. Carlisle said it could have been the reason for his anger issues before Seth came to stay with him. Things all made sense with the diagnosis, but he hated it, nonetheless.

Seth installed a motion sensor on the back and front door that chimed on his phone. There was no way he'd have *that* scare again. His daily runs had stopped. Instead, he worked with improvised weights and calisthenics to keep his cardio engaged. He made sure Gomer stuck to his dad like glue. The dog understood his task and followed Chester everywhere.

Labels went on every drawer in the house, especially the kitchen. He was doing anything to help Chester navigate the space that had once been second nature. Still, by the fourth day, Seth was running on fumes.

After Chester had gone to bed, Seth sat alone on the porch. Gomer lay sprawled at his feet, tail thumping softly every now and then as if to say, *Still here.*

The stars were out, sharp and brilliant in the South Dakota sky. Seth leaned forward, elbows on his knees, eyes fixed on the distant horizon. It was too late to call Allison. He didn't want to wake her. And if he were honest, he didn't want to make his loneliness her burden. The truth was, he hadn't realized how *lonely* caregiving could be. Or how *guilty* normal emotional responses to his father's disease made him feel. The smallest frustrations built up, like bricks stacked in a line. He hated the way he reacted when Chester asked the same question over and over. The impatience that shouldn't be there but sometimes was. He hated the resentment that crept in when he wanted an hour to himself but couldn't get it. And he hated that he missed the old version of his father. The version that didn't get along with him. The version that was stubborn, self-righteous, and pigheaded. The one that remembered what day it was and that his mom had passed.

The screen door creaked open behind him, and Chester stepped outside, squinting into the night. "You coming in soon, boy?"

"Yes, sir," Seth replied quietly. "Just needed a minute."

Chester nodded like he understood. Maybe he did. Maybe those flickers of clarity hadn't gone out just yet.

"You know," Chester said, his voice low, "I never said thanks."

Seth looked up, surprised. "For what?"

"For coming back. For dealing with me and … things."

"You don't have to say thanks, Pops."

Chester crossed his arms and looked down at him. The same way he always had, stern and strong. "Maybe not," he said. "But I should. And I'm saying it now. Thank you."

Seth stood slowly.

They faced each other in silence, only the rustle of wind in the trees filling the space between them. Then Seth did something he'd never done before. He reached out and placed his hand on his father's shoulder. And took the leap he'd never dared take before.

"I love you, Pops," he said. "I don't think I've ever said that out loud."

Chester's eyes dipped, his jaw tight. "I feel the same, boy. Don't say the words, but I feel the same." His voice cracked, and tears shimmered in his eyes. "I hate that you have to see me like this."

Seth cleared his throat, struggling to hold steady, to keep the emotion from clogging the words between them. "Don't be, Dad. I'll take care of you. You taught me how to be a man. How to carry my weight and the weight of others."

Chester's eyes cut to him, sharp again. "Others?"

"Delbert," Seth said simply.

Chester gave a small smile. "Man is dumber than a box of rocks. Used to be smart, though. You know what he was like?"

Seth shook his head. "No, sir. I didn't meet him until after the accident."

Chester nodded. "Yeah, I knew that." He sighed and glanced at Seth again. "When I can't anymore … you check on him, all right?"

His father had asked him to watch out for Delbert before. But Seth didn't mind repeating the answer. "That's a promise, Pops."

Chester sniffed and looked toward the house. "Good. We should go in. Getting chilly out here. Making my nose run."

Seth fought back the lump in his throat. *Cold, he'd go with that.* "Yeah. Mine, too. Let's go in."

Seth glanced back and waited for Gomer to walk into the house after his father. He looked at the brilliant stars in the sky and said a prayer of thanks for the moment of clarity, the memory, the words, and the emotion that was choking him. He'd carry this moment and those words in his heart for the rest of his life.

CHAPTER 11

*A*llison jumped at the sound of her back door creaking open. The sun had barely risen, casting a faint golden glow across the town. It was six thirty, and she wasn't expecting anyone yet.

Kayla Thompson stepped inside with a gust of cold morning air, startling her.

"Oh my God, girl," Allison gasped, clutching her chest. "I thought you were the homeless woman!"

Kayla froze mid-step, looked down at her leggings and oversized hoodie, then lifted an eyebrow.

"Well, I realize I'm not dressed to the nines, but *homeless?*"

Allison laughed, the tension breaking. "Coffee's

done. Pour us a couple of cups, would you? I'll be there in a second."

Kayla moved toward the small kitchen counter in the back break room and began prepping their morning coffee. It was a ritual now and one of the comforting routines of living and working in a town like Hollister. Kayla's little shop, built next to the bakery, was half seamstress studio and half second-hand boutique. There wasn't much she couldn't mend or track down, and her store had become a staple in a town where convenience was king and Walmart was hours away in Spearfish.

While most folks would run down to Rapid or Belle if they needed something, having Kayla next door saved people time.

"So, why'd you call me homeless?" Kayla asked, passing a steaming mug to Allison's side of the table.

"I didn't *call* you homeless, silly," Allison replied with a grin as she washed her hands at the sink. "There's a homeless woman taking food out of my trash can."

Kayla paused, cup halfway to her lips, then turned, brows raised. "Are you sure?"

Allison nodded as she dried her hands on a towel. "Yeah. I saw her the other day. She disappeared before I could say anything, but I know what I saw. Seth saw her, too. I've been leaving real food in there at night, wrapped in plastic. It's always gone right after I put it out. I haven't caught her, but she returns the insulated bag. It's sitting by the bakery door every morning."

Kayla had fixed her the coffee, just the way she liked it. She sat at the small table and cradled her cup between her palms, warming them.

"Okay. Number one: Who's Seth? Number two: I left for two weeks for that quilting exhibition in Chadron and a jaunt over to Minneapolis, so I'm completely out of the loop. And number three: Someone took clothes out of my donation box." Kayla took a sip before continuing, "Not that I mind. I don't make much off those secondhand pieces. But I knew there were some clothes in there. Alex told me someone had dropped a few items off, but he hadn't sorted them into the store yet. When I went to check, it was empty."

Allison frowned and chewed her bottom lip thoughtfully. "I put in a fleece-lined hoodie. An old one, but it was warm. Left it on top of the trashcan the second night. It was gone, too. It's getting cold at night. Maybe she needed something else to keep warm," she said quietly.

"Like I said, I don't care. It just made me stop and go, *wait, what?* But if we've got someone homeless ..."

She trailed off, eyes flicking to Allison. "Here? In *Hollister*? I mean, how does that even happen? With the churches, the outreach stuff, people pitching in?"

Allison shook her head slowly. "I didn't recognize her. Neither did Seth."

Kayla lifted her hand in the air like she was in second grade, then took another long sip before she said, "Allison. I have a question."

Allison laughed. "Yes, Kayla?"

"Who the hell is Seth?"

"Seth Hansen. Chester Hansen's son. He came back to take care of Chester."

Kayla's eyes widened slightly. "Oh, that's right! I heard he was coming back. But Alex said he thought Seth had to leave real quick after showing up? Something like that?"

Allison nodded. "Yeah. Had to go get his military working dog from back east. But both of them are back for good now."

Kayla leaned back in her chair, cupping her coffee like a lifeline. "I needed this so bad."

Allison took a sip of her own. The warmth spread through her. It was a needed hit of caffeine since she'd been baking since four thirty. These small breaks with Kayla were comfortable and part of her routine. They meant a lot to her, and she cherished the time with her friend.

"Anyway," she said, "I told Ken about the woman. He's going to have the deputy keep an eye out. When Seth and I were talking with Ken and Sam at the diner, they wondered if maybe the woman came through with some people who passed through a couple of weeks ago. Maybe she's trying to get away from something or someone."

Kayla tilted her head. "Abusive relationship?"

Allison nodded. "That's what Sam was thinking. I only got a glimpse of her, but she was covered in bruises."

Kayla's face darkened. "That kind of thing doesn't happen much out here, does it?"

Allison thought of a few ranchers she knew with sharp tempers, but none who'd ever laid a hand on family, or at least not that anyone had ever dared say aloud.

"No. It really doesn't," she said. "And if it *did*, it wouldn't stay hidden long." She blinked as she thought of the Koehlers. Yeah, they were the exception to the rule. Gregg was the only one still around; all he did was work. That had been a messed-up family, for sure. But they'd escaped their terror of a father.

Kayla nodded slowly, her expression serious now. "Well, if she's here, she's hiding for a reason. And we don't turn our backs on people around here. You let me know if there's anything I can do."

"I will," Allison said quietly.

Outside, the early morning sun finally began to lift over the eastern fields, casting light across the tiny town of Hollister. Shops were just starting to wake, their windows glowing with life, and in this quiet, connected community, secrets never stayed secrets for long.

"You know how people talk around here," Allison said.

Kayla nodded. "Boy, do I ever."

"Has Edna seen this girl?" Allison asked.

"I didn't ask," she admitted. "But if she *had* seen her, you and I both know she'd have been the first one here with the details."

Allison chuckled. "That's true."

Kayla's eyes lit with sudden excitement. "Oh! Do you know what I got?"

Allison narrowed her gaze, playful suspicion written all over her face. "Do I *want* to know what you got?"

Kayla grinned. "I got a book on Bigfoot sightings."

Allison blinked. "What?"

"Yup! All about where he's most likely to be seen in the continental United States. I picked it up while I was in Chadron. There's this eclectic little store just off Main Street. I wandered in, saw it, and couldn't resist. Anyway, I'm going to have Alex leave it on Edna's table one morning when she meets with Kate and the girls. I think it will be *fun*."

Allison rolled her eyes as she finished wiping down the counter. "You know, I used to enjoy winding her up, but now? Sometimes it's just sad. How could she actually *believe* there's a Bigfoot?"

Kayla shrugged. "I don't know. That last photo she showed us? It really did look like something. Maybe not Bigfoot, but not quite human either and definitely not just an animal."

"It was a smudge on the lens," Allison said dryly.

Kayla raised a triumphant finger. "It was a digital camera, *Lucy*. Explain that."

Allison shook her head with a half-laugh. "I don't have the time or the inclination to get into Edna's Bigfoot conspiracy theories."

"I do," Kayla said cheerfully. "I think the woman

has a great hobby, and honestly? We should support it."

Allison grinned, relenting. "Speaking of support, how'd the quilting exhibition go?"

Kayla leaned back in her chair, hands wrapped around her coffee mug like it was gold, stars practically shining in her eyes.

Allison laughed at the sight. "Oh, no. I know that look."

"Girl," Kayla sighed, "there were *so many* new machines. Dozens of them. All doing the most fantastic things I've *ever* seen. I have to have one. Except ... I need like five thousand dollars."

"That's all?" Allison teased.

Kayla huffed, but her eyes danced. "Not the point. But maybe I'll find a used one online in a year or two. Oh my goodness, it would change everything. You should've seen what this one model could do. It stitches the top and the bottom layers perfectly, has auto-threading, a bobbin sensor, and an overhead light that doesn't cast *any* shadows. None. Zero." She paused, eyes misty. "One day. One day, I'll get one of those fancy machines."

Allison lifted an eyebrow, her mind already turning. Alex had talked to her before about how Kayla rarely spent money on herself, and how she saved every spare penny, always pouring it back into the shop or her customers.

"What's the name of it?" Allison asked casually.

Kayla launched into a detailed explanation about brand, features, model number, and stitch patterns, all of which made Allison's eyes nearly cross. But her friend was in heaven, so she listened. Twice.

As soon as Kayla stepped out to open her store, Allison scribbled the machine's name down on a slip of paper. She'd give it to Alex later when she dropped by Gen's diner at lunch. He might not be able to afford the top model, but he did love to spoil his wife.

She had just finished arranging her last batch of golden, buttery croissants when the bell above the front door jingled.

Allison looked up and smiled. "Hey, Amanda."

Amanda Marshall breezed in, her smile as wide and warm as the South Dakota prairie sky. Her long braid swung over her shoulder as she stepped inside.

"Hi, Allison! Do you have my order ready?"

"I sure do," Allison said, heading into the walk-in cooler.

She returned with a large light purple box filled with freshly baked bread bowls, the yeasty scent filling the room.

Amanda accepted the box with gratitude. "Thank you so much. And while I'm here, can I get a couple of your strawberry pies? If you have them in stock?"

"I actually have three in the walk-in. I was planning to bake blueberry tomorrow."

"Then I'll take all three," Amanda said cheerfully. "Jewel and Zane are coming out with the twins before school starts."

Allison tilted her head. "Wait. School already started, didn't it?"

Amanda smiled. "Oh, the twins are homeschooled. They do their coursework in Denver during the year, part of a co-op there. They're both ahead of their grade levels. One excels in math, the other in science. And they spend summers back home."

"Where's home?" Allison asked.

Amanda waved her hand vaguely. "Back in the Carolinas."

Allison caught the subtle signal that said, *Don't push*. So, she didn't. "I'll pop back and grab those pies for you. Be right back," Allison said with a smile as she turned toward the walk-in cooler.

She stepped inside and pulled out two strawberry pies, placing them gently on the prep table before returning for the last one. As she secured the lids and made sure each box was wrapped with care, the bell above the door chimed.

Frank Marshall stepped into the bakery, the light behind him casting long shadows across the polished floor.

Allison grinned. "I see you've got your weekly stash of taffy," she teased, nodding toward the small brown paper bag in his hand.

Amanda laughed, brushing her fingers across her husband's sleeve. "Please don't let your mom ever run out of that. I found a source for some high-protein taffy, but this man refuses to eat it."

Frank lifted the bag as if defending a long-held tradition. "Ain't nothing wrong with this taffy. Been eating it all my life. Probably gonna eat it till the day I die."

Amanda's hand slid around his back. "Well, that won't be for a long, long time. Do you understand me?"

Frank looked down at her, smiling softly. "Yes, dear." He bent and kissed her forehead, the kind of small, familiar gesture that spoke of years of devotion.

Allison moved the pie boxes toward the counter and lined them up neatly. "I'll just put it on your bill," she said as she rang them up.

"Thank you so much," Amanda said warmly. "You're gonna have to help me with these," she added, glancing at her husband.

"I will," Frank replied, shifting the weight of the boxes as he accepted them from Amanda. "But I've got a question first."

Allison looked up, her hand pausing over the register. "What can I help you with?"

Frank tilted his head toward the front window, and when she looked in that direction, she saw Delbert sitting outside the general store, watching Main Street with the same focus he gave every slow-moving vehicle that dared to roll through town.

"Where's Chester?" Frank said. "Is he still coming down here every day?"

Allison glanced at the clock and then out the front window and nodded. "Oh, he should be here any minute."

And just like that, Seth's truck pulled down Main Street, easing in from the highway. She caught sight of the dusty hood and the big black German Shepherd sitting alert in the passenger seat.

"There he is." She smiled.

The truck rolled to a stop in front of the general store. Gomer jumped out the passenger side, landing gracefully before circling the truck to wait at the rear door. The dog stood in a protective hover as Chester shuffled out, slow but steady. Gomer scooted back just far enough to give him space, then moved in line beside him.

Seth waited until his father was upright and headed for the bench before he shut the door and followed behind. Once Chester had settled with Gomer curled at his feet, Seth turned toward the bakery.

"Sharp dog," Frank said as Amanda unwrapped a piece of taffy and popped it into his mouth. "Thank you," he said as she laughed and walked across the bakery to the trash can.

Allison smiled. "He should be. He's a retired military working dog. Tracking and drug detection were his specialties. Seth said he was a kennel master. Whatever that means. Apparently, the more rank he earned, the further they pushed him from the dogs."

Frank's eyebrows lifted, and he nodded. "Heard that from Ken."

She smiled as she watched Seth ambling down the street. "From what I gather, he didn't like being behind a desk. When they retired Gomer because of arthritis, Seth put in for adoption and flew out to bring him home himself."

"Is Seth sticking around?" Frank asked, chewing

his taffy slowly while Amanda balanced the smaller boxes atop the larger one he now held in his arms.

"Yeah. His dad ... isn't doing too well. Seth's his full-time caregiver now."

Frank grunted. "Alzheimer's?"

Allison's smile was tinged with sadness. "Yeah. That's what the doctors confirmed. Seth thinks part of the meanness that hit before he came home was from a UTI. The doctor speculated the same. Chester's been on antibiotics, and he's settled quite a bit since then. He's calmer. Seems more like himself."

Frank nodded thoughtfully as Amanda stepped to the door and opened it wide. She asked, "Ready to go, dear?"

Frank glanced down at the boxes piled in his arms. "I don't think I've got room for anything else."

Amanda laughed and held the door for him. "Bye, Allison. See you next week."

"Take care," Allison called, waving.

She looked past them just in time to see Seth nearing the bakery. But he stopped as Frank said something, and the two men stood for a moment talking. Frank gestured once toward the general store, then toward Seth's truck. Amanda, meanwhile, unloaded the boxes from Frank's arms into the back of their vehicle.

Seth nodded, shook Frank's hand, then resumed his walk to the bakery.

Allison took a moment to catch her breath and wipe her hands on her apron.

Seeing Seth walking toward her under the South Dakota sun, the horizon wide and the sky endless behind him, made her heart skip.

CHAPTER 12

Today had been busier than most days Seth spent with his father. Before heading into town to let Chester whittle with Delbert at the general store, Seth had driven out to the stockyards on the south edge of Hollister. The buildings there were a patchwork of corrugated metal and weathered wood but well constructed and solid. The air was thick with the scent of hay, manure, and diesel from passing livestock trailers. Dr. Kate Wells ran her veterinary practice in a converted barn at the far end of the lot.

Seth hadn't expected to know the vet, but when he stepped into the office, he froze in the doorway.

Kate Johnson, now Wells, he assumed, looked up

from her desk and blinked in astonishment. "Oh my God. Seth?"

He laughed, just as shocked. "What in the hell are you doing in Hollister?"

She pushed up from behind her desk and rounded it without hesitation, wrapping him in a hug. "I could ask you the same thing. I thought you were stationed in Germany. Last I heard, you were at Ramstein."

"I was. Didn't know you were from South Dakota."

"I said Colorado, right?" She laughed, pulling away.

"You did."

"Well, my dad's from here. Hollister born and raised. You remember Lawrence Johnson?"

"I do. He was in my class." Seth blinked. "Wait. You're Lawrence's sister?"

Kate nodded, grinning. "Sure am."

"Of all the things in the world," Seth said, shaking his head. "Small world. Blessing said to say hello."

"Oh, you've met her. She's ..."

"Unusual," Seth supplied.

"She has the sight," Kate said. It was a challenge for him to doubt it. He didn't.

He nodded. "Probably."

Chester, seated off to the side with Gomer at his feet, raised a brow. "Thought we were here to get the dog checked, not flirt with the vet."

Seth rolled his eyes. "Kate, do you know my father, Chester Hansen?"

Kate extended her hand with a warm smile. "Mr. Hansen, we haven't officially met, but I'm Tegan Wells' wife."

Chester stood, took her hand, and gave it a brief shake. "Here to get the dog's paw looked after. My fault he got it cut."

"Oh, is that so?" Kate bent down and offered Gomer her hand. "Hello there. You look familiar." She looked up at Seth. "Is this Gomer?"

"Sure is. A little gray around the muzzle, and he's stiff with arthritis. I have a sixty-day supply of meds, but I need to make sure we're on the best routine. Here's the list of what he's on." He pulled a sheet of paper from his pocket. "When they retired him, I made a trip back east to get him. I have a soft spot for this dog."

Gomer offered his paw instinctively when Kate extended her hand, taking the medication sheet with the other before she chuckled and ruffled the scruff behind his ears.

"Well, I have a soft spot for him, too."

Seth crouched beside her. "He cut his paw in the pasture almost two weeks ago, now. It was healing just fine, then I noticed some swelling. It's hot to the touch, and the salve I've been using isn't helping."

He pulled a small jar from his pocket and handed it to Kate. She studied the label, then stood. "That's a good general solution, but we may need to need to go with a full antibiotic. Let's get him up on the table and take a closer look."

It took only a few minutes to examine Gomer's paw. Kate cleaned the wound, applied a more potent antibiotic ointment, and wrapped the paw securely.

"I'll send the prescription refill over to the pharmacy in Belle," she said as she finished the wrap. "I have a couple of days' worth I can give you until you can get to Belle. You'll want to watch for swelling, but this should take care of it. As far as the arthritis meds, they're what I would prescribe. Keep him active, but no running or jumping. Anything hard on his joints will make him hurt more. I'd like to take x-rays sometime soon to get a baseline. Maybe you could stop in one day next week."

"Thanks. We'll do that."

Kate smiled. "It was great seeing you, Seth. We'll have to get you out to the house for dinner sometime. You do remember Tegan, right?"

"I vaguely remember him. I was a lot older than you guys."

She rolled her eyes. "Older by what, five years?"

Seth laughed. "Yeah, but when you're a senior, the freshmen seem a world away." He scratched Gomer behind the ears and stood. "Thanks again, Kate."

"Anytime." She looked at him, a little more seriously this time. "Seth, do you have a minute?"

"Sure. Dad, can you take Gomer to the truck? Time to go see Delbert."

Chester nodded and stood slowly, taking Gomer's leash. Seth watched them, the image of loyalty and quiet dignity framed by the open stockyard door and the endless sky beyond.

Chester grumbled as he shuffled down the hallway, Gomer glued to his side like they'd been partners for life. "I'm not disabled," Chester muttered. "Delbert's dumber than a box of rocks."

Kate chuckled as she opened the door for them. Seth followed, grinning at his father's theatrics.

"But he's your best friend," she pointed out with a teasing smile.

Chester sighed dramatically. "Says a hell of a lot about me, doesn't it?"

Seth laughed. "Yeah, Dad, it does. It says you're one hell of a guy."

Chester snorted and kept walking, the dog matching his step. It was as if the dog had always belonged to the man.

Seth waited until they were out of earshot, then moved to a nearby window. He watched until his father opened the correct truck door, helped Gomer inside, and settled in to wait. The sight calmed him just a little.

"I have to stay where I can see him," he said, still looking out the window. "He's got Alzheimer's. Sometimes he gets confused."

Kate sighed softly beside him. "I'm sorry to hear that. I know it's gotta be hard on you."

Seth shrugged. "It's harder on him. What did you need?"

"Do you still have your security clearance?"

"Yeah, I should for at least another six months. They just renewed it before I got out."

"What level?"

"Top secret. Why?"

Kate gave a small nod. "Well, I know there's a position for a kennel master here in Hollister."

Seth's brow furrowed. "Excuse me? What are you talking about?"

"Have you heard anything about the Marshall Ranch?"

He offered a cautious nod. "Enough to not ask what you're talking about and not admit knowing about it."

"Right," she said, smiling. "Anyway, Mr. Marshall is looking to start a kennel. Some of the work happening at the ranch and elsewhere could really benefit from dogs trained in tracking and explosive detection."

"That right?"

Kate nodded. "I'll make a call tonight, but don't be surprised if Mr. Marshall reaches out."

"I'm not sure I can take anything on right now." He nodded back toward the truck. "I'm my dad's full-time caregiver. It's only going to get more time-consuming."

Kate rested a hand on his back. "I understand. But this town … It's one hell of a community. You don't have to do it alone. If you need help, just ask."

Seth smiled and shook her hand again. "Kate, it was good seeing you. I honestly had no idea you were from Hollister."

"Only during the summers." She laughed. "I lived with my mom in Colorado growing up."

Seth nodded. "And I worked out at the ranch every summer. Rarely came into town. That's probably why we never crossed paths."

"Well, we'll fix that now. I'll talk to Tegan and give you a call. Your number's in Gomer's file. I'll shoot you a text if I hear anything from Mr. Marshall."

"Sounds good. But as I said, I'm not sure I can commit to anything."

"Just listen to what he has to say. That's all. It won't hurt."

"That's true." Seth turned back to the window. "I've gotta go. Chester's getting out of the truck."

"Take care, Seth."

It took a little coaxing, but Seth managed to get his father back into the truck. He reminded him that they were headed to sit with Delbert at the general store. That whittling bench had become Chester's sanctuary. As soon as he had a piece of wood in his hand and Delbert beside him, it was as if the fog in his mind lifted just a little.

With his father settled and Gomer lying in the shade under the bench, Seth made his way across Main Street to Allison's bakery. He was looking forward to a few quiet minutes, and maybe a few smiles, with the woman who'd slowly begun to occupy his thoughts during the quiet late at night. Hell, who was he fooling? He wanted to kiss the woman until neither of them could breathe. She made his blood run so hot that cold showers were no longer helping. Yeah, they hadn't made the next move, but God help him, he wanted to, and the way she reacted to him, he could tell she wanted him, too. He smiled to himself. He'd figure out a way to have some quality alone time with her. Somehow, some way, he wanted more than the fantastic conversations, stolen looks, flirtatious innuendos, and cold showers.

He hadn't made it to the front door before an older man stepped into his path.

"Seth Hansen?"

Seth blinked, his mind jerked back from his less than moral thoughts. "Yes, sir."

The man extended a hand. "Frank Marshall. Wondering if I could bend your ear for a minute."

Seth shook his hand. "Of course."

Frank nodded toward the truck. "Sometime when you're not busy. Maybe Monday? One o'clock? Over at the diner? We can get a table away from everyone and talk."

"I'd like that, sir. I just spoke with Kate Johnson, excuse me, Wells, and she mentioned the situation."

"Then I'd like to give you the facts and get your thoughts."

Seth nodded. "Yes, sir. I can do that. I'll see you at

one on Monday, but only if my dad is doing okay that day. He controls my schedule."

"Good man." Frank smiled, then turned to help his wife load up the last of her bakery order. Seth watched them for a moment before stepping inside, ready to see Allison and grateful for the moment of normal in a day that had already held more shock than anything else.

Seth opened the back just as Allison braced her knees to lift a bulk bag of flour from the bottom shelf in the storeroom.

"You really gonna try to lift that on your own?" Seth's voice drifted in, rich and full of amusement.

Allison let out a huff and looked over her shoulder. "I've been doing this a while, Seth Hansen. I'm stronger than I look."

"I don't doubt that," he said as he stepped closer. "But there's strong, and then there's sensible. Let me get it."

Before she could argue, he bent and effortlessly lifted the fifty-pound sack, settling it against his shoulder like it weighed nothing.

Allison stood and wiped her hands on her apron, watching him carry it through the prep kitchen with practiced ease.

"Where do you want it?" he asked.

"Next to the mixer," she said, moving to clear a space.

He set it down gently, then straightened and grinned at her. "You're baking for the entire county this week?"

"Pretty much. I've got two birthday orders, a church breakfast, and I'm starting to bake the rest of the items for the Fall Festival. Don't worry, though, I'll be free on Saturday."

Seth leaned a hip against the counter and crossed his arms. "Saturday, huh?" The thought of them spending some time together, alone, in the dark hadn't been on his mind much. Just every other second of the day. He smiled.

"Yeah," she said, opening the bag and pulling out a scoop. She looked up at him. "You remember our date, right?"

He tilted his head. "You mean the one I've been thinking about every day since we set it? Yeah, I remember."

That earned him a smile, small and soft. "Good," she said, cheeks coloring faintly. "I've been looking forward to it."

He took the flour scoop from her and pulled her into his arms. "Me, too," he said. Then, more quietly, "More than I probably should."

Allison looked up. "Why do you say that?" Her eyes moved from his to his lips.

He smiled, and he knew he looked like a predator, but he didn't care. "Because this thing between us? Feels like the kind of thing that doesn't just go away."

The kitchen stilled for a moment. Outside, a pickup rolled past, the tires crunching gravel on Main Street. Inside, the air felt warmer, closer.

"I don't want it to go away," she said, pressing closer against him. "But I've got baggage, Seth. I'm a mess half the time. And I overthink everything."

He held her tighter.

"Good," he said. "Then we'll match just fine." He lowered his head and kissed her. The flame he'd imagined leaped into a raging fire. He pulled away. "Damn, you are delicious."

She blinked up at him. "It's the sugar."

He laughed and shook his head. "No. It's you." He dropped for a kiss again. The sweetness of her wasn't artificial, it was real, and it was addictive as hell. When he drew away, she sighed and leaned against his chest. "Are you sure? I know I want this, but are you sure?"

He tightened his arms around her. "You have baggage, and well, so do I. I've got a dad who sometimes forgets his own name and a house that smells like antiseptic and wet dog. My life isn't perfect either, but I still want this with you."

Allison tipped her head up and looked at him. "I do, too."

They stayed like that, wrapped in each other's arms, warm and certain, the silence stretching easily between them. Finally, Allison cleared her throat.

"Well," she said, "if we're trying this, you should know that you signed up to help me lift five more bags of flour."

Seth groaned, but he was smiling. "That's a lot of dough, Sanderson."

"You don't scare easy, Hansen. Do you?"

"Nope," he said.

Allison huffed a laugh, brushing a streak of flour off her cheek with the back of her hand. "Remember, you offered, big guy. I didn't force you."

"Remind me of that when I can't feel my back in the morning," he teased and released her after a quick kiss. He walked over to the flour and hefted it without any problem before taking it over and setting the bag down gently near the mixer.

She handed him a scoop and opened another bin. "If you're looking for sympathy, you're not gonna find it in here. Try Edna. She believes Bigfoot eats hunters and sympathy for breakfast."

Seth chuckled and took the scoop from her, brushing his fingers over hers for half a second longer than necessary. "So, we're still good for Saturday?"

"Of course," she said, glancing at him from under her lashes. "Unless you're planning to cancel on me for another hot date with your dad and Delbert."

"Nope. You're top of the list," he said, his voice quieter now. "I've been looking forward to it."

Allison gave him a soft smile, then turned back to organizing pie tins on the counter. "Good. Me, too."

For a moment, the only sounds were the soft hum of the refrigerator and the occasional clink of metal against metal. The quiet wrapped around them, but it wasn't awkward. It was comfortable. Settled.

Seth stepped closer, dusting his hands on a dish towel before reaching over and straightening one of the pie pans. She turned slightly, her face inches from his. Her eyes widened just a little, but she didn't step away.

Seth hesitated, just for a beat, then leaned in and pressed a kiss to her lips.

It was gentle. Not rushed. Not possessive. Just enough.

He felt her intake of breath. Then the softest hint of her leaning into him, her mouth parting willingly for him. He pulled her against him. His need overtaking gentleness. He searched her mouth with a passion he didn't try to curtail. He wanted this woman. He needed her in a way he couldn't express with words. So, instead, he used his tongue, teeth, and hands to let her know how much the connection between them meant to him. He lifted away quickly, and before she could speak, before he allowed her thoughts to catch up with the moment, he smiled. "See you tomorrow," he murmured, brushing a thumb over her cheek where a little flour lingered.

He spun and went out the back door with a casual wave. Not his best move, but if he didn't get out of there, they'd end up on the floor with flour bags as a mattress. Not necessarily desirable or sanitary, for that matter. As he hit the bottom of the steps, he heard her call out, "Did not see that one coming! I like the surprise attack."

"Good, I'll keep you guessing," Seth called back and headed to the general store. He'd sit with Delbert and his dad for a while.

* * *

THE PORCH BOARDS creaked softly as Seth leaned back in the old wooden rocker, the one Chester had built before Seth was even born. It groaned under his weight, but it held, just like it always had. Gomer stretched out on the rug beside him, muzzle resting on his paws, his breathing slow and even. The breeze carried the scent of sage and dry earth, and the stars above scattered across the inky sky like someone had spilled a box of silver dust.

He sipped from the chipped enamel mug in his hands, black coffee still hot enough to keep him company. It had been a long day. A full one. A heavy one.

Kate had thrown him for a loop. Seeing her again after all those years, in a vet clinic of all places, right here in Hollister, felt like one of life's strange little full circles. She hadn't changed much. Still sharp, still quick to smile, and still dead honest. The way she'd looked at him when she mentioned the job at the Marshall ranch … yeah, she knew exactly what she was offering.

And then Frank Marshall stopping him? That wasn't a coincidence. That was orchestration or at least confluence.

He scratched the back of his neck, thinking about the conversation. It hadn't been pushy, just ... interested. Respectful. But underneath the small talk and easy tone, Seth knew Frank Marshall was sizing him up. Calculating. That offer might be a lifeline or a snare. He hadn't decided which yet. The snare would be his need to take care of Chester. He wasn't going to ditch that responsibility. He couldn't.

Still, none of that had rattled him half as much as Allison had.

He smiled, slow and involuntary, the memory of her mouth under his still buzzing through his veins.

It hadn't been planned. Hell, it had barely even felt like a choice. One minute, she was working, her cheeks warm, her hair pulled back in that loose, careless way that made her look even more beautiful. Next, she was standing close. Like close enough that the scent of cinnamon and sugar clung to her skin.

So, he'd pulled her in and kissed her. Rough, real, and fucking addictive. The chemistry between them was real.

Now, sitting there with the night wrapped around him, Seth felt content, even in the swirl of questions surrounding his father.

He didn't know what tomorrow would bring.

Chester's good days came and went like clouds drifting over the prairie. Some days were clear. Some were lost in the fog. And Seth was still trying to figure out how to be a son, a caregiver, and maybe, just maybe, a man falling in love.

But tonight?

Tonight, he had those delicious memories.

CHAPTER 13

The scent of slow-cooked beef and fresh-baked rolls drifted on the evening breeze as Allison stepped up onto the porch, balancing a tray covered in mismatched dishtowels. The sun hung low in the western sky, casting golden rays over the prairie. Crickets had begun their nightly chorus, the sound low and rhythmic beneath the distant creak of the porch swing.

"I come bearing gifts," she called, nudging the screen door open with her hip.

Chester looked up from the small wooden table where he sat, a deck of cards spread before him like he was preparing to storm a casino. His brow lifted, skeptical.

"That better be food and not another damn rabbit-food salad," he grumbled.

Allison laughed, adjusting her grip as the screen door slapped shut behind her. "No salad. I made pot roast with carrots, baby red potatoes, and soft yeast rolls. There's extra gravy and a cherry cobbler that needs to be cooled on the counter."

Chester gave a low, satisfied grunt. "Woman, you just got yourself upgraded to sainthood."

Seth stood from where he'd been adjusting an old folding chair beside Chester. His flannel sleeves were rolled up to the elbows, revealing forearms sprinkled with sawdust. "Let me take that," he said, reaching for the tray.

Their fingers brushed, and a small static moment sparked between them before Allison released her hold. "It's hot," she murmured, watching his hands instead of his eyes.

He nodded, the corner of his mouth twitching up in a quiet smile. "I got it."

Dinner was spread out over the little porch table with real plates, real silverware. No paper napkins. No shortcuts. Just home. The pot roast flaked apart at the touch of a fork, the potatoes were creamy, the rolls buttery and still warm. A pitcher of sweet tea sat between them, already beading with condensation.

"You ever play Spades, Allison?" Chester asked as he wiped a smear of gravy from his plate with a roll that had at least a half-inch of butter slathered on it.

"I can bake you under the table," she said with a grin. "But I'm not much of a card shark."

"She's got a baker's precision," Seth said, helping himself to seconds. "I bet she could clean up if she wanted to. Maybe even count the cards."

"Hell, you don't need to count if you've got charm." Chester winked. "Back in my day, I won half my games and all my arguments that way."

Seth groaned around a mouthful of roast. "Don't encourage him. Pops, you growled your way through life. You didn't charm your way."

"I like her," Chester muttered, tearing his roll in half and soaking up the last of the gravy. "She feeds me and doesn't fuss. That's damn near perfect."

Allison arched a brow. "High praise, coming from you."

Chester popped the bread into his mouth and said around the food, "Don't let it go to your head."

She smiled and poured more tea into Chester's glass. The meal was full of banter and warmth. Laughter filled spaces that used to echo with silence.

Even Gomer lay peacefully at Chester's feet, tail occasionally thumping when Allison passed by.

When the last bite of cobbler had been scraped from the dish and the dishes were packed back onto the tray, Allison gathered her things and took them to the car. She returned to find Chester rising from his chair, rubbing his lower back with a wince.

"I'm turning in," he muttered. "Gomer, with me."

The dog rose instantly and padded after him.

"Don't go falling in love on my porch," Chester called over his shoulder, not bothering to look back.

Seth chuckled. "He's a charmer, isn't he?"

Allison settled beside him on the porch swing, tucking her legs beneath her. "Ever fallen in love on this porch?"

"Not so far."

The screen door slapped shut behind Chester. A moment later, the porch lights flickered on, casting a soft yellow glow over the swing. The air had cooled just enough to make the warmth of a coffee cup feel comforting.

The land around them was silent except for the whisper of wind through the grass and the hum of distant insects. The sky stretched wide overhead, deep blue and velvet soft, the stars just beginning to show.

They sat there in the hush, coffee cups cooling between their hands, neither one rushing the moment. Allison glanced sideways at him, her expression shifting. "I wanted to talk to you about something," she said softly.

Seth turned toward her, his attention sharpening. "Okay."

The porch swing creaked beneath their weight, a soft rhythm that matched the cadence of the crickets chirping in the tall grass just beyond the fence. A distant owl hooted from a cottonwood tree, its cry carrying across the open prairie. The sky overhead had shifted from blue to indigo, stars piercing the dusk one by one. Fireflies blinked lazily near the fence line, floating like bits of light trying to find their way home.

Seth leaned back, his arm stretched along the backrest. The warmth between them was steady, companionable, but Allison's voice drew tighter now, worry curling around her words as she shared her worry about the woman they'd both seen. She still hadn't been located. But Allison had been feeding her, and clothes from the donation box next door had gone missing.

"Did you tell Ken?" Seth turned to look at her

when she'd finished, concern sharpening his features.

"I called him again, and he came by," she said, her voice softer now. "I'm scared for her. She hasn't picked up any food in two nights." She exhaled, frustrated. "I don't know what to do, but she needs help. Can you think of anything? It's going into fall, and we get snow early up here. Granted, that's a month or so from now, but still ..."

Seth nodded, his brow furrowed. "Not sure. I mean, she could have left. I can try to track her with Gomer. I'd need something she'd worn. Something with her scent. He's a damn good tracker. I'll talk to Ken about it."

"Would you? The insulated tote I use to put food out for her. She's handled it. Would that work?"

"I can't promise anything, but we can try."

Her shoulders sagged a little, tension leaking out as she looked over at him. "Thank you."

"Of course," he said, but his eyes flicked back toward the screen door. "But I'd need to see if I could get someone to stay with Chester. I wouldn't want to leave him alone."

"I'd stay with him." Her answer came without hesitation. "I wouldn't mind."

They fell quiet, the swing easing them back and

forth with a gentle sway. Coffee cups sat cooling on the rail beside them, forgotten now. The stars above were brighter, the land stretching around them in every direction, open and quiet and unhurried. It was the kind of silence that invited honesty.

Allison shifted, pulling her knees up and wrapping her arms around them. "Do you ever feel like … maybe you broke something in yourself, and you're not sure how to put it back together?"

Seth turned to her, his profile carved in moonlight. "Every day. Then I realized some things break for a reason and don't need to be put back together."

She smiled, small and tired. Not because it was funny, but because he actually understood. "I used to hold onto Ken," she said, her voice dropping lower. "Not because I loved him. I didn't. But the idea of someone else having him made me panic. Like I'd lose something. But I didn't want him anymore and still couldn't let go."

Seth didn't interrupt. He waited, letting her find her words, for which she was grateful. She wanted this relationship to work, so she wanted to be completely honest with him. "I wasn't proud of it," she continued. "I was over him. We were just … in each other's orbit. But I'd reach out when I was lonely or thought he was looking elsewhere. We were never sexually intimate; I couldn't do that to myself, let alone him. I believe that's reserved for a person you believe you might have a future with ... at least in my opinion. I knew we didn't have a future." She looked down. "Now I realize all that time I dangled a relationship in front of him, it wasn't about him. It was about me. I didn't want to feel like I was forgettable."

Seth nodded, slow and steady. "You're not."

Her gaze lifted to meet his. There was no hesitation in his words, no flinch. Just truth.

"I've been figuring out a lot of things, doing some hard work on boundaries. Figuring out why I feel like I'm invisible sometimes."

"How's it going?"

"Better," she said, then paused. "I still have moments when I flinch at normal things. Like, someone being nice to me, and I wonder what they want. Ducking people so I don't take up space but feeling like crud when I do that to myself."

"Like when you tried to avoid me at the hospital?"

She huffed, a little embarrassed that he'd caught that. "Ah ... saw that, did you?" Seth nodded, and she admitted, "Yeah. That was a prime example. Or, on the other end of the spectrum, I get scared that I'll lose myself if I care too much. But I see it now. The patterns. I name them, and since I can identify what I'm doing, it helps."

He leaned forward, elbows on his knees, his voice quiet. "That's a hell of a lot braver than most people ever get."

"I want to be someone who's healthy, you know? Not just for someone else. *For me.*" She hesitated, her fingers tightening as she clasped her hands together. "But if I'm ever in something real again …" She swallowed, heart pounding, "I want it to be built on truth. Not fear. Not habit. I guess that's why I'm telling you all of this. Because to me, this is real."

Seth looked at her, really looked. There was weight in his eyes. Not pity. Understanding. Like he knew what it meant to want to get it right this time, even when everything inside you was afraid to try.

"I think this is real," he said. "I'm not smart enough to have all the answers, but I'll be one hundred percent honest with you, always."

The words settled between them like the promise it was meant to be. The space on the porch felt warmer somehow. Safer.

Allison smiled, not because she had the answers but because, maybe, she didn't need to.

She shifted again, leaning her shoulder lightly on

the back of the swing. The wood was warm against her back. She didn't press him. Didn't fill the silence. She let it settle, let it breathe.

Seth finally spoke, his voice low and rough. "I was married once."

Allison turned her head toward him, surprised. "You were?"

"Yeah. For about six months. Well, I lived with her for six months. The divorce took over a year. We were both handlers for military working dogs. Met in training, got together fast. It was one of those whirlwind things that felt right in the middle of all the chaos." He grabbed his cup from the rail and ran a finger around the rim. "She cheated. Repeatedly. We worked different shifts, and I was the last one to figure it out, which probably says something about my intelligence."

Allison didn't say anything. He needed the space to let it out, just like she had earlier.

"I think I held onto her because we understood the job. Because she was familiar when nothing else was. But she didn't respect me or us. Didn't care the way I thought she did."

He looked over at her, jaw tight. "That wrecked a lot of things inside me. Trust. Pride. Man, both of those took massive hits." He gave a short, bitter laugh. "I spent the next twenty years alone. I dated, but nothing serious. Then I retired and came back stateside. Two months later, my dad started slipping ..." He trailed off, staring into the darkness.

"You came home," Allison said softly.

"Yeah. He was confused when I got back. He was growly and mean. God forbid anyone know Chester Hansen couldn't handle his life."

"Was he always like that?"

"Proud? Stubborn as hell?" Seth gave a small nod. "Yeah. He wasn't a bad dad, not exactly. Just ... hard. Distance was his way of loving people. And silence was his version of showing you he trusted you. If he didn't have to bark at you, you were golden."

Allison sensed the ache in his voice wasn't sharp or bitter. He just seemed tired and worn down.

"I resented him for a long time," he said. "Still do, sometimes. But now? Watching him slip ... It's like the worst parts of our history don't even matter anymore. I keep the best morsels of our time together in here." He touched his chest, over his heart. "I just want to keep him safe. Give him some dignity."

When he looked out at the land again, Allison followed his gaze. The fields stretched quiet and silver in the moonlight.

Seth continued, "So, yeah. Married and divorced when I was barely able to drink legally. A decorated career handling and training dogs. And now, back in my hometown, I care for a man who never once said, 'I need help,' until a couple of days ago." His laugh was low, rueful. "So, we can both attest to having a bumpy road. Good thing we know where the ruts are now."

Allison reached over and brushed her fingers against his. It wasn't a grab. Just a touch. Gentle. Steady. And she wasn't afraid to make the move, which was pure heaven. Her inner demons seemed to vanish around Seth. "You don't have to drive that route all alone," she whispered. "Whatever this is, and whatever the ending, I'm here for you. You don't have to do this alone."

Seth's eyes met hers, quiet and searching. Something settled there in his eyes, something that looked a lot like hope. "Yeah," he said. "I think I'm starting to believe that."

He leaned in.

The kiss wasn't hesitant. It wasn't rushed either. Just a slow, claiming brush of lips that deepened as the silence wrapped around them. Her hand slid to his jaw. His arm curled around her waist.

She ended up in his lap, her body pressed against

his, the swing groaning under the shift. His hands moved to her hips, his mouth trailing heat against her throat. The air between them grew electric. Breathless.

Desire flared, sharp and white hot and undeniably real.

Allison's breath hitched as Seth's mouth returned to hers, more insistent this time, less careful. His hands slid under her shirt, rough palms against the curve of her waist, anchoring her to him. Her heart beat so hard she felt it in her throat and heard it in her ears.

"This isn't slow," he murmured against her mouth, his voice low, gravel-edged.

She didn't pretend to misunderstand. "I know," she whispered, fingers gripping his shoulders as if to ground herself. "I don't want to go slow with this. Not right now."

"Then we'll go slow later."

She nodded. "Later, much later."

"Next year?"

She shook her head. "Next century."

"That's a long time." He smiled down at her.

"Take a hint, Hansen." She lifted her eyebrows at him.

* * *

THAT WAS ALL HE NEEDED.

Seth stood, one arm under her thighs, the other around her back. The porch swing rocked violently as he lifted her off it, but he didn't pause. He carried her inside, his steps fast and sure, booted feet thudding against the old wooden floors. The door clicked shut behind them, Gomer glancing up from his place near Chester's room before settling again with a huff.

Seth didn't speak as he crossed the living room, his focus entirely on her. He pushed open the door to the guest room and stepped inside, kicking it closed behind him.

Allison's back met the mattress, her breath rushing out of her as he followed her down. His mouth was on her neck, her jaw, her collarbone. She arched into him, pulling his shirt loose from where it was tucked into his waistband.

Every kiss, every touch, was confirmation that this moment was happening. And it wasn't careful or tentative anymore. It was all-consuming. Unleashed. He'd never wanted anything so badly. His body ached for her, and the nights spent thinking of this moment didn't compare to the real thing.

His fingers brushed the hem of her shirt and slid higher, pausing just beneath the lace of her bra.

"Allison," he breathed against her skin, voice hoarse. "Tell me if you want to stop. You say the word, and I stop." He'd stop. There was no question there. Whatever she needed, he'd make sure she got.

With her eyes locked on his, she shook her head. "I want this."

His hand stilled, and his gaze searched hers, a flicker of tension passing through the heat.

Then she said it, soft but clear. "I need to tell you something."

Seth froze above her, his body humming with restraint, breath coming hard.

"I'm still a virgin," she whispered.

The room fell quiet. The only sound was the ticking of the old clock in the hall and the distant call of a night bird from beyond the window.

Seth blinked. His brow drew down. His mind tried to make that statement compute, but he couldn't. Disbelief swamped him until he stared at her and saw the truth.

"You're...wait, you're serious?" His voice dropped, raw and reverent all at once. "Allison..."

Color rushed to her cheeks. "I know that's probably not what you expected. But it's true. I've come close before, but I never followed through. It never felt right."

Seth leaned back slightly, his weight shifting to his forearms as he looked down at her, stunned. "You could've said nothing. I wouldn't have known."

"I didn't want to do that," she whispered. "Not with you. Honesty, always honesty."

His eyes softened, and he reached up, brushing a strand of hair back from her face with aching gentleness. "Jesus, sweetheart." He exhaled, his forehead lowering to rest against hers. "You're … you're giving me something you've never given anyone else."

Her fingertips trailed down his arms. "This, us … It feels right, doesn't it?"

For a long moment, he didn't move. Just held her, forehead to forehead, their breath mingling in the space in between. "This feels perfect, and we'll take our time," he whispered. "We're here, together. Right now. No pressure. No rush. Just us."

The woman he held planted the biggest compliment and one hell of a serving of responsibility on him with those simple words. He didn't want this to be a mistake for her. He needed this relationship to be solid and true, and he knew his intention toward her was honorable. Hell, he could see himself with her for the rest of their lives, but he wouldn't scare her with that revelation.

Seth hovered above her, his eyes searching hers. He needed to make sure, one last time, that this wasn't something she'd regret. "Babe," he whispered again, barely more than breath, reverent and unsteady. "If I do this, I need to do it right."

She reached up, her palm against the side of his face, thumb brushing over the edge of his jaw. "Then don't be careful with me, Seth. Be real. I need real. I …" She closed her eyes. "You are who I want. Who I need."

That did something to him. Unleashed something quiet and reverent that had been chained up behind all his restraint. He lowered his mouth to hers with aching need and every ounce of tenderness he could find. Their kiss was slow, sensual, and hot. He was no longer tentative. His hands moved beneath her shirt again, warm against bare skin as he lifted the fabric inch by inch, pausing only to make sure she was still with him.

She was. God, she was. They both leaned into touches, to the dance that spun them higher and higher. She shivered at his touch. The soft moans and sounds of her pants filled the room. They were the sexiest sounds he'd ever heard. Her shirt landed somewhere on the floor. Then her bra, undone with steady fingers and care that he prayed told her he wasn't just undressing her; he was memorizing and mapping every inch of her body. Her hot, tight, gorgeous body.

"You're beautiful," he murmured, his voice rough even to his own ears. "You always were." He'd always admired her. Her laugh, her personality, but he knew he was leaving Hollister the first chance he got, and besides, she was Ken's. Or so he'd thought. Now, he could stare at her beauty because she was his. All his, and she was giving him the most beautiful present he'd ever received. She was giving him herself, and he would honor that present forever.

Her chest rose and fell beneath his gaze, vulnerable and naked, but she didn't flinch, and he prayed she understood the reverence he was trying to give her. His hands slid over her hips, down to the waistband of her jeans, and then paused. His mouth was on her again, whispering promises against her neck.

"We'll go slow," he said, even though he was barely holding himself back. "I need you to feel everything. No rushing through it."

"I want to feel everything," she whispered, her arms pulling him closer. "I want you."

The room was filled with the soft sounds of

breath and the rustle of sheets. His shirt joined hers, then her jeans, then his. Piece by piece, they shed the barriers between them. The air was warm and heavy, filled with the scent of night air and skin.

He kissed her like she was something he didn't dare break because she was a present, and she was safe in his arms. She would always be safe with him. He reached over to the nightstand, grabbed his wallet, and pulled out a condom.

"Why?" she panted.

He stopped and looked down at her. "Protection against pregnancy."

"I'm on the pill." She took the condom and tossed it off the bed.

"Probably for the best. That thing is five or six years old."

She laughed, and he smiled down at her. The humor died, but the passion between them engulfed them white hot and urgent.

When he entered her, it wasn't without hesitation. He paused, kissed her cheek, her jaw, her temple. God, it was painful to stop, but for her, he'd endure hell. "You okay?"

"Yes," she whispered. "I want this, Seth. I want you."

And then there was no space left between them.

It wasn't perfect, but it was real. They laughed and sighed. There were awkward moments that melted away as they found a rhythm. Was it the perfect coupling? God, no. But it was good, and the depth of the honesty between them was powerful. It was the type of intimacy that broke the holds of the past and shone a light on the future.

Seth held her gently because this woman mattered, and she'd taken up a place in his life with ease. He treated her like the precious gift he believed she was. And when she cried, just a little, he kissed the tears from her cheeks.

When they were both quiet again, tangled in each other beneath the worn quilt and the soft moonlight coming in from the window, Seth spoke first. "I can't help but feel you just changed everything for me," he said, voice bare and honest. He needed her to know what he was saying was the truth.

Allison didn't answer right away. She just curled closer to him, fitting into the space his body made for her. She whispered, "I think you changed everything for me first. You saw me."

Outside, the wind whispered through the prairie grass. Inside, two people who had lived through a rough and rutted past found something neither thought they'd get. A fresh start.

CHAPTER 14

The morning sun filtered through the gauzy curtains, painting soft gold across the room. Outside, a rooster crowed somewhere. Allison stirred first, blinking against the light. Her body ached in a good way, muscles warm and stretched in places that hadn't been used quite like that before. She smiled before opening her eyes, the memory of the night clinging to her skin like the scent of Seth's cologne.

He was still beside her, and she admired the picture of him. Bare-chested, hair tousled, his arm heavy around her waist, anchoring her to the bed like he had every right to keep her there. And you know what? He did have that right. She'd given that to him. She searched her mind and her heart for any regrets, but smiling, she knew there were none. Seth filled the empty spaces in her life. Would the future be perfect? No, but who expected perfection? She wanted real and honest, and she found that with him.

She eased out from under the quilt as gently as she could, tugging one of his old flannel shirts from the chair near the bed and slipping it on. The hem nearly hit her knees.

She padded barefoot toward the kitchen, intending to make coffee or at least start breakfast, but she'd barely crossed the living room when the hallway creaked and Chester appeared, shuffling out in a rumpled Army T-shirt and flannel pants, hair sticking out in all directions. Gomer was glued to his side.

He squinted at her, rubbing one eye with the back of his hand. "You here already? Drove all this way so early?"

Allison blinked. "Uh..."

He grunted and shuffled past her toward the counter. "Damn early to be feedin' a man, but I won't complain. You bring food?"

She bit back a laugh, cheeks warming. "Actually, I'm using what you have here."

"Smart." He gave her a side-eye glance, then

blinked like he was trying to piece together a puzzle, but it wasn't making a picture. "Thought I heard you come in, but then I thought I must be dreamin'. Hell, I didn't even hear Seth get up."

"He's, uh …" Allison tucked a piece of hair behind her ear, glancing back toward the hallway. "Still sleeping."

Chester reached for the coffee canister, muttering under his breath as he scooped grounds into the pot. "Well, if you're makin' breakfast, I prefer my eggs over medium to hard done. None of that runny yolk nonsense."

She smiled, tension leaking out of her shoulders. "Got it."

He turned to look at her again, brow furrowing. His eyes dropped to the oversized flannel shirt she wore. That look continued to be puzzled, which she was sorry for and happy about at the same time. Then he looked away, cleared his throat, and fussed with the coffee filter.

"Not my business," he muttered. "You want to feed a man before daylight and wear a shirt as a dress, hell, that's between you and society. Seen it all in my day."

Allison covered her grin with the back of her hand, her cheeks burning with heat.

Behind her, bare feet whispered against the floorboards, and Seth's hand landed lightly on her back as he stepped up beside her. "Morning, Dad."

Chester didn't look up. "Mornin'. You sleep good?"

Seth paused. "Yep."

Chester poured water into the coffee maker. "Thought I heard thunder last night."

Seth blinked. "Thunder?"

"Uh-huh. Lotta rumbling."

Allison turned bright red. She could feel the heat creeping higher, and her pale complexion and red hair didn't help cover up her embarrassment, not at being with Seth, but at Chester's words. If the man ever put two and two together, she'd melt into the linoleum. Puddle, splat, gone.

Seth looked like he was going to choke on air. "Think the weather's passed now," he managed to say finally.

Chester looked up, one eyebrow raised. "What has?"

"Ah, the weather? All the rumbling?" Seth supplied.

"We had weather? Didn't hear it." Chester moved toward the table with a grunt and dropped into his seat before reaching for the paper. "Are you making breakfast? Eggs, girl. Medium to hard cooked. Don't like runny yolks. Nasty stuff, that. And maybe some toast."

Allison turned to Seth once Chester was buried in the crossword.

Seth leaned in, voice low and full of teasing amusement. "You okay?"

She nodded, smiling even as she whispered, "Your dad thinks I came over at sunrise to cook breakfast."

Seth grinned. "Let him. We're adults."

And just like that, the awkwardness was gone. Not erased, but softened by the simplicity of the morning, the man who'd raised Seth, and the quiet promise that last night didn't need to be hidden, it just didn't need to be explained.

Allison rolled up her sleeves and reached for the pan. "Eggs. Medium to hard over and toast, coming up."

* * *

ALLISON SMILED ALL the way back into town. Seth would be by shortly so Chester could sit out front of the general store with Delbert, even though it was closed on Sundays. That was their routine. It grounded Chester, gave him something to look forward to. She pulled around to the back of the bakery and put the truck in park. That was when she noticed the woman sitting on the steps to her bakery.

Slowly, Allison turned off the engine and climbed out of the cab, careful not to startle the figure hunched in layers of mismatched clothing. The woman looked up, her expression guarded and weary.

"Are you okay?" Allison asked gently, approaching with slow, steady steps.

The woman shook her head. She was trembling, arms wrapped tight around herself.

"Can I help you?" Allison pressed softly. "Let me take you upstairs to my apartment. You can get a shower, and we'll figure this out. It doesn't matter what kind of trouble you're in. As long as you're not a serial killer or anything."

The woman rolled her eyes faintly, and Allison took that as a good sign.

"I'm not a killer," she said.

Allison crouched down beside her, voice steady. "Then let me help you. My name's Allison. I live here, but I think you already know that."

The woman gave a slight nod.

"Are you in trouble?" Allison asked, standing and offering her hand.

"I don't wanna talk about it. But I need help."

"Then you've got it. People in this town, they're the best. No one here will hurt you. I promise."

They walked up the stairs together, and when they reached the top, Allison unlocked the door and helped the woman step inside.

"What do you need first? Food, water, or a shower? I'll bring you some clothes to wear."

The woman's eyes scanned the cozy space. "A shower. Then maybe some medicine. I can't stop shaking. I think I've got a cold. Or a fever."

"Probably because you've been outside and not eating well," Allison said.

The woman nodded weakly.

"Are you strong enough to take a shower? There's a bench in there if you get dizzy."

"Yeah. I'll be okay."

Allison led her to the bathroom. "There's shampoo, conditioner, and soap in there. The towels are clean and on the rack. I'll grab you some clothes." She turned to leave but paused. "What's your name?"

The woman's eyes widened with fear.

"Hey, now," Allison said quickly. "You don't have

to tell me. It's okay. As I said, we're not going to hurt you here. I'm just trying to help."

The woman wrapped her arms tighter around herself, glancing nervously up and down the hallway.

"Loretta. My name is Loretta."

"That's a pretty name," Allison said with a soft smile. "Go ahead and take your shower. I'm not calling anyone. I won't say anything to anybody. I want you to feel safe. My boyfriend will be here in about an hour or so. You've got plenty of time to shower and eat. He won't hurt you either. He's prior military, and he'll protect us."

Loretta gave a wary nod. "The one with the dog?"

Allison nodded. "Yeah. That's a military working dog. Or he was. He's retired now."

"I heard the conversation."

Allison's brow knit. "How?"

Loretta rubbed her forehead. "I've been hiding under your boardwalk. That's how I knew there were clothes in the deposit box. And how I could get food out of your trash can."

Allison blinked, stunned, and her mouth fell open. "How long?"

"I'm not sure. Two, maybe three, weeks."

Allison took a slow breath and nodded. "Okay.

You go on and take your shower. Take as long as you like. I'll leave the clothes right outside the door so you can feel safe. Lock it if you want."

Loretta gave a grateful nod and shuffled into the bathroom, closing the door behind her.

Allison leaned back against the hallway wall, exhaling hard. "Holy smokes," she whispered, rubbing her face. Her thoughts spun, but one rose to the top.

What the hell do I do now?

Food first. And something to drink.

The woman, Loretta, was nothing but skin and bones. It was no wonder she was sick. Exposure to the elements, a lack of food, and no clean place to wash up would wear anyone down. Allison wasn't even sure if the bruises still existed beneath the layers of grime, but now that she'd made contact, maybe she could gently talk Loretta into letting her call Ken. Or better yet, Zeke Johnson. The town's doctor would absolutely take her in pro bono. That's just what they did here.

Allison bit her lip, pushing off the wall the moment she heard the water start. The soft hum of the pipes and the patter of the shower brought a flicker of relief. It was a step in the right direction.

She rummaged through her drawers, frowning as

she tried to gauge Loretta's size. Even with her lost weight, the woman was much lighter. Allison found a pair of drawstring leggings and the smallest T-shirt she owned. She added a sports bra and, thankfully, had a new package of underwear she could offer. Then she placed everything in a neat pile on the floor outside the bathroom door and popped back to her room to grab a pair of pink fluffy socks and an oversized hoodie. The way Loretta had shivered, it had probably been a long time since she'd been warm.

In the kitchen, she pulled out a container of the chicken rice soup she'd picked up from the diner. It was always made fresh, and it always hit the spot. While warming it in a saucepan, she slid a couple of slices of sourdough into the oven. As the bread began to crisp, she checked on the clothes. The door creaked open, and a hand reached out to grab the pile. Then the door clicked shut again.

Allison waited another twenty minutes before Loretta finally emerged. Her hair was damp, combed back, and she looked … less haunted, though exhaustion still hung around her like a storm cloud.

"I borrowed your comb," she said quietly.

Allison waved her off. "Anything you need, you've got. Are you ready to eat something?"

Loretta nodded. "Yeah."

She followed Allison into the kitchen, her movements sluggish, shoulders hunched. Allison handed her a steaming bowl of soup and two warm, thick slices of sourdough slathered with butter. The woman took a few careful bites, then leaned back, arms wrapping around herself again.

"I don't think I can eat much more."

"That's okay," Allison said gently. "You've got time to ease into it. How about I get you a blanket? You can sit on the couch and rest. We can talk a little later."

Loretta nodded, and when she stood, she wobbled. Allison rushed forward, catching her before she could fall.

"Whoa there. Come on, let's get you comfy." She guided her to the couch and returned with a thick, soft blanket. Kneeling in front of her, Allison tucked the blanket over her legs. "Listen," she said, meeting Loretta's eyes. "I'm fine with you staying here. I'm fine with feeding you and keeping you warm. But I really think Dr. Johnson needs to take a look at you. Those bruises ... you've been through something. And you nearly passed out just now."

"I don't wanna cause any trouble," Loretta whispered.

"It's no trouble, I promise you. And while we're at it, we could maybe let Ken, the sheriff, know you're here."

"No." The word cut through the air, sharp and sudden. Loretta bolted upright, nearly knocking Allison back. "No police. No police whatsoever."

Allison raised her hands, palms out. "Okay. Totally cool. No police. No Ken. I get it."

Loretta was shaking, her eyes wide and filled with panic. Tears welled up and rolled down her cheeks. "I haven't done anything wrong," she said again, her voice cracking. "I haven't done anything illegal. I haven't hurt anyone."

"I believe you," Allison said softly, stepping closer. "And we're not going to call anyone unless you want us to. But I'd still like Doc Johnson to take a look at you. I'm worried about you, Loretta."

Loretta's arms hung at her sides, one awkwardly crooked, and Allison wondered if her shoulder was hurt.

"Can I just sleep?" she whispered. "Just sleep without shivering, without worrying that I'm gonna be found?"

"You're safe here," Allison said firmly, pointing toward the couch. "Do you want a pillow?"

"No. I just wanna lie down."

"Then lie down. When you wake up, we'll talk more. We'll go at your pace. Okay?"

Loretta nodded, curled onto the couch, facing the back cushions, and pulled the blanket up to her shoulders. Within moments, her breathing slowed, and soft snores filled the quiet apartment.

Allison stood there for a long while, watching her sleep. Then she turned and made her way into the kitchen. Before she could start clearing away the dishes, she reached for her phone and typed out a quick message.

Could you come up to my apartment when you get to town?

I have a window we can see Chester through.

She hit send, knowing Seth would come.

Something told her this woman was in a hell of a lot of trouble.

CHAPTER 15

Any and every time Seth needed to be somewhere quickly, Chester decided it was the perfect moment to slow everything down. Seth had texted Allison to let her know he was leaving, but then Chester had insisted he needed to take an anvil to the barn and back. There was no talking him out of it.

So, Seth walked with him to the barn, then back. Only then was he finally able to get Chester into the car and load up Gomer.

"Where are we going?" Chester asked.

"We're going to town, Pops. Remember? You're going to go whittle with Delbert."

"Dumber than a box of rocks," Chester muttered, looking out the window.

Seth smiled. "That's right, Dad," he said as he turned onto the highway toward Hollister.

"Who was that girl who was here this morning?"

"Her name is Allison, Dad. Allison Sanderson. The Sandersons own the general store."

Chester nodded thoughtfully but didn't say anything. They drove in silence for about five minutes before Chester asked again, "Who was that girl who was here this morning?"

"My girlfriend, Dad. Allison Sanderson."

Chester frowned and turned to him. "You have a girlfriend?"

"Yeah, Dad, I do."

Chester let out a whoop. "About damn time, son."

Seth laughed at his father. "You've been waiting for me to get a girlfriend, old man?"

"Been waiting for you and your sister to settle down. Sarah is married," Chester said. Then he looked at Seth, eyes a little sharper than usual. "Right?"

Seth nodded. "Yep. She has two little girls. That's why she couldn't come to stay with you. That's why I said I would."

Chester scowled. "Don't need no damn babysitter."

"No one ever said you did, Pops," Seth replied

softly. And he meant it. He would never make his father feel like a child.

They turned into Hollister, the town nearly silent. Delbert was slowly making his way to the bench out front of the general store. One or two townsfolk strolled along Main Street, but everything else was shuttered. Nothing was open on Sundays, a rhythm as dependable as the prairie wind.

But if anyone needed anything, well, everyone knew who to call to get what they needed.

Seth pulled up in front of the general store and waited for his father to get out of the truck. Gomer hopped down and stepped beside Chester like he'd done it a thousand times. Once his father was settled on the bench and Delbert had taken his usual seat, Gomer sat loyally at Chester's feet, the perfect guardian.

Seth handed Chester the block of wood he'd been whittling on earlier, along with his old pocketknife. "Here you go, Pops."

Chester turned the wood block over in his hands and frowned. "I think you were making a bird," Seth offered.

Delbert glanced over. "Yup. A bird. We always make birds."

Chester rolled his eyes. "I know that, Delbert. My

problem is I don't know what kind of bird I was making this time." He looked up at Seth. "I might forget things, but I know what I whittle."

"Birds. Always birds." Delbert nodded. "Stuck in a rut."

"Better a rut than the alternative," Chester grunted.

Delbert glanced at Chester. "Alternative will come sooner or later. No fighting it."

"Watch me," his father growled.

Seth chuckled and tapped his dad's shoulder. "Okay, Dad. I'm gonna walk over to Allison's. I can still see you from there. If you need anything, just stand up."

Chester scowled. "Don't need no damn babysitter."

"I know, Dad. Just saying." Seth turned and walked toward Allison's place. He hadn't been to her apartment above the bakery before, and he looked forward to it. He took the stairs two at a time and at the top was just about to knock when the door opened.

Allison stood there, and before she could say a word, Seth grabbed her by the waist, pulled her in, and dipped his head. "Hello, beautiful. It's been too damn long."

Laughing softly, she shushed him and slipped out the door, shutting it behind her. Seth looked from her to the closed door. "This wasn't what I expected. And why are we being quiet?"

"Loretta is sleeping on the couch."

"Who's Loretta, and why is she sleeping on your couch?"

"Loretta is the woman I've been feeding. She was sitting on my steps when I got home this morning. She's not doing well. She swears she hasn't done anything illegal, and I believe her. She's terrified, Seth. I don't know of what, but I really think Doc Johnson needs to take a look at her."

"We need to call Ken. If she's afraid of something—"

Allison held up her hand. "No, we don't call Ken because she asked me not to. No police."

Seth frowned. "I don't like that." Actually, it set his nerves on edge to the point of grinding. "Why doesn't she want the police involved? It isn't like we're going to turn her over to the same people who did this to her."

"We don't know what happened to her, so we have to find out. I'm *not* calling Ken. But I told her you were coming. And you have law enforcement training, right?"

Seth nodded. "And?"

"Well, maybe you and I can talk to her. You can figure out what's going on. Then you can talk to Ken, and I won't have broken my word."

Seth raised an eyebrow. "Oh, you are a devious one, aren't you?"

Allison shrugged. "I used to be. Trying really hard not to be that anymore. But I think we'll have to take matters into our own hands. She could barely eat anything, which tells me she's either really sick or she's been out in the elements too long. But I've been feeding her, so I'm leaning toward sick. You know what I mean?"

"I do. And I'm hoping whatever she has isn't contagious." He gave her a pointed look.

Allison's eyes widened. "I didn't even think about that."

"I know." He gently tucked a strand of hair behind her ear. "You were only worried about her. You wanted her to be safe."

She nodded. "Yeah. She's sleeping now and probably will be for quite some time. Would you come back tomorrow and talk with her?"

"I'd be happy to. As long as you get Doc Johnson up here now to make sure she's not going to be contagious or infect you with something. I couldn't handle that." His thumb brushed her cheek tenderly.

She leaned into his touch. "Did I tell you I had a really good time last night?"

Seth smiled. "Not in so many words, but there were a few actions I picked up on."

She wrapped her arms around his waist and looked up at him. "You know, Seth, you keep talking like that, I'm gonna think you like me."

He kissed her, slow and soft. "You keep holding me like this, and you're gonna know how much I like you."

Chuckling, she slid her hands down to squeeze his backside. "Oh? Then I'll tell you I think you're special."

"So are you. See, we're communicating." He leaned in for another kiss. "Call Doc Johnson," he murmured against her lips.

"I will."

"I'm going to wait at the store. We're not leaving until I see he's been here."

Allison sighed and leaned into him. "I really did have a good time, Seth."

"So did I. We'll have to do that again."

"I wouldn't object in the slightest." Allison chuckled.

He kissed her once more, then turned her around and gave her backside a playful swat. "Go call the doctor."

She spun to look at him, eyes dancing. "Tease."

"Do you want more of that, young lady?" Seth raised a brow.

She laughed and shrugged. "Maybe." Then Allison winked at him and walked inside, closing the door.

Seth groaned. The woman would be the death of him. He smiled and started whistling on his way down the steps. But, man, what a way to die.

He headed back to the store and sat down on the steps, absently petting Gomer while his father and Delbert talked about nothing and sent chips of wood scattering across the boardwalk. Seth couldn't hear what they were talking about, but the tone was good-natured. Gomer, content and calm, lay at Seth's feet, ever the quiet sentinel.

Across the street, Seth spotted a tall blond man walking behind the bakery with a tall woman whose curly blonde hair bounced with every step. He figured that had to be Doc Johnson. Relief settled over him. Allison had followed through. His woman never hesitated when someone needed help. He stopped and smiled at that thought. His woman.

His phone buzzed in his pocket, and when he pulled it free, he smiled.

Doc and his wife are here. He's talking to her now and going to check her out.

Seth tapped a quick reply:

I saw them. Still out here with Chester.

Allison responded with a simple red heart. He smiled and slipped his phone back into his pocket.

A truck rumbled onto Main Street from the highway. Seth vaguely recognized it and watched as it pulled into the garage. Frank Marshall climbed out alongside another man, who Seth didn't recognize. Together, they wrestled a hydraulic lift from the truck bed. Frank exchanged a few words with his companion, then crossed the street and sank down on the steps beside Seth, his knees propped on his elbows.

"Figured we could talk today if that's okay with you," Frank said in a low voice. "John, my ranch manager, is going to stay over there, and I don't think your father or Delbert can hear us from this distance."

Seth nodded. "We can do that."

Frank glanced his way. "I'm going to take your gentleman's handshake on the fact that you'll sign an

NDA. Don't have it with me today, but what I'm about to tell you is confidential."

Seth met his gaze. "Mr. Marshall, I have top secret clearance. It's still active. If what you're about to tell me affects national security, you have my word I won't say a thing."

"That it does, son. That it does."

"Then you have my word." Seth extended his hand, and Frank shook it firmly.

"Guardian Security has a presence on my ranch," Frank said.

Seth chuckled. "Best kept non-secret in the world."

Frank pulled a piece of taffy from his shirt pocket, unwrapped it, and offered one to Seth before popping his own into his mouth. Seth accepted the candy with a grin and did the same.

"That being said," Frank continued, "the powers that be are looking at training dogs to deploy with our teams. Not all the teams. Some are too specialized, but teams working in urban warfare or search and rescue missions. Dogs like yours could change the outcome of an operation."

Seth nodded. "Early detection saves lives."

"That's what I figured." Frank tilted his head

toward Gomer, who was dozing beside Seth's boots. "Tell me a little about this one."

"He's a tracker and a drug dog. His nose is his superpower."

Frank chuckled, nodding thoughtfully. "Always wondered how they train for that. Can't exactly hand him a textbook."

Seth grinned. "Nope. It starts before they even learn to sit. First thing is selecting the right dog. You need one with drive, confidence, and curiosity. You want a dog that'll chase a tennis ball through fire and won't flinch at a gunshot. Focus is essential. Gomer passed all those tests in about twelve weeks. But that initial selection? That's everything."

"So, what's next? Obedience?"

"Exactly. We nail down the basic commands like heel, down, stay. It's not just about manners. It's how we build trust. These dogs have to listen, even when everything around them is chaos. Once that's solid, we imprint them on a target scent. Could be narcotics, explosives, even people."

Frank raised an eyebrow. "Imprint?"

"Means we pair the scent with something they love, which is usually a toy. For Gomer, it was a tug towel. He'd catch a whiff of cocaine, and boom, he was ready to play. Over time, he learned that finding the scent meant a reward. One plus one equals two, and these dogs quickly figure out the math. Then we ramp up the complexity. We hide the training aid in harder places, throw in distractions, conflicting odors, and different environments. Keeps their brains sharp."

Frank nodded and gestured to the field beyond the mechanics' garage. "What about tracking?"

Seth leaned forward, elbows braced on his knees as he scanned the dusty road that cut through Hollister. The scent of weathered wood and sunbaked prairie grass drifted on the breeze, mixing with the faint tang of machine oil from the nearby garage. The low hum of insects rose from the dry field beyond the mechanics' building.

"Gomer was trained to track after he'd been certified in drug detection. He was between handlers, and I had time. He was a natural. All he wants to do is please his handler. In training, we teach them to follow ground disturbances and the skin cells a person sheds when they move," Seth said, nodding toward the golden field. "At first, it's short tracks with food drops or play as rewards. I prefer play, and food rewards are growing less common nowadays. Then we go longer. We throw in cross-tracks, wind shifts, and real-life variables. Gomer could follow a track that was several hours old. Still might be able to, honestly. He's slower now with arthritis, but that nose still works."

Frank nodded slowly, gaze resting on Gomer. "What does he do when he finds something?"

"He alerts," Seth answered. "We train dogs with a passive alert. Meaning they'll sit or freeze and stare at what alerted them when they find something. You never want an aggressive alert. Not when you're talking bombs. Scratching at a live explosive isn't exactly a great idea."

Frank gave a dry laugh. "No, I reckon not."

Seth shifted, leaning against his thighs. "After all that, we certify them. Blind tests. Vehicles, luggage, buildings. No help from the handler or anyone in the scenario, not even the slightest look. We have QC people watching the handler just as hard as the certifier is watching the dog. Dog's got to do the work on its own. If not, it can cost lives. Theirs and ours."

Frank studied him for a long moment. "Sounds like the handler and the pup have a hell of a bond."

"It's true. It develops fast. They trust us, and we trust their noses more than our own eyes."

Frank looked out toward the field again, sagebrush swaying under the big sky. "So, to start this program, you'd have to know where to get the right kind of pups."

Seth nodded. "That part's not hard. There are breeders who specialize in working dogs."

Frank scratched his jaw. "I'm looking for someone who knows how to build that kind of bond the right way. Someone who knows how to train a dog, not break one. I won't stand for abuse. Not on my land."

"It's not my way either, sir," Seth replied firmly.

"I need someone like you out here. Not just for the dogs, mind you, but to help train the handlers. We want good people. Could you do that?"

Seth's jaw tightened, and he rubbed the back of his neck before casting a glance toward Chester, who was still happily whittling beside Delbert. The old man's laughter carried faintly across the dirt street.

Seth looked back at Frank. "I appreciate it, sir. I really do. But I can't."

Frank's brow lifted. "Why not?"

Seth exhaled and lowered his voice. "It's my dad, sir. He needs me. Full time. It's not just memory lapses anymore. He gets turned around. Sometimes forgets where he is. I won't go into detail, but he can't be left alone."

Frank nodded solemnly. "Heard he had Alzheimer's."

"Yeah. And it's progressing. The meds help, but they're not stopping it."

A quiet settled between them, filled only by the breeze rustling through cottonwoods that lined the distant creek bed.

Frank reached into his pocket again, drew out another piece of taffy, and handed it over. Seth took it, waiting until Frank unwrapped his before doing the same.

"You got him on insurance?" Frank asked.

"Yeah. He's also on Medicare. Doesn't mean much when he needs someone with eyes on him all day."

"Well, here's a thing," Frank said as he leaned in. "I know the state offers in-home nursing services during the week. Monday through Friday. They've got contracts with solid folks. His insurance would cover most of it. Wouldn't cost you much, if anything."

Seth frowned. "I don't know, sir. Leaving him alone makes me twitchy."

Behind them, the town remained still. The flags on the lampposts by the post office fluttered a bit. Somewhere, a dog barked in the distance, and the faint scent of someone grilling carried faintly on the breeze. It was just another quiet day in Hollister, but Seth's world was anything but quiet.

Seth didn't answer right away. Instead, he watched his father laugh with Delbert, Gomer's head resting on his paws like a contented old soldier. The weight of responsibility tugged at him, but so did something else... a possibility.

He leaned forward, elbows braced on his knees as he scanned the dusty road that cut through Hollister.

"Son, you wouldn't be leaving him alone. You'd be giving yourself a break," Frank said, his voice softening. "You think I don't see it? Hell, you think your dad doesn't see it? There's a strain in your shoulders, son. Your face shows it. You love that man, but being a full-time caregiver will eat you alive if you don't carve out space for yourself. And maybe space for yourself and Allison."

Seth snapped a glance in his direction.

Frank almost smiled. "I'm old, not blind. That woman lit up when talking about you. But back on topic. You'd still be home every night. Maybe start with part-time if that helps. From what I've gathered, you're good at this work. And I may or may not have reached out to people I know in the military to verify that fact."

Seth exhaled, voice rough. "I've been holding it together. Taking it one day at a time."

"You don't have to do it alone," Frank said. "No shame in accepting help. Shame is burning out before your dad really needs you the most."

That hit Seth hard, like a punch to the breadbasket. He'd heard that statement in so many variations. Perhaps he needed to let it sink in. He nodded slowly, swallowing the lump that had risen in his throat. "Will you let me think about it?"

"Sure. You take your time," Frank said, clapping a hand on his shoulder and stood up. "But just know the door is open. And you'd be doing more than training dogs out here. You'd be giving some of the nation's finest an edge. An edge some of them desperately need."

The weight of that statement settled around Seth's shoulders. It was one of the reasons he loved working with the dogs. It was extraordinary what they could do for the humans they served. But only if the humans treated them right.

He stood and looked at Frank. "I'd have a condition to your offer, should I accept it, sir. One you need to consider before you agree because it's non-negotiable."

Frank Marshall looked at him, his brow furrowed. "Like what?"

"If you send a handler in for training, and he doesn't mesh with the dog, or I don't feel he's a good fit for the animal, I'll wash him out of the program. Immediately. He goes back to his team, no harm, no foul, but he does not stay with my dogs."

Frank smiled. "I knew I liked you, son. That's a guarantee. You call me when you have an answer."

He reached into his shirt pocket and pulled out a white card with nothing but a cell phone number hand-printed on it.

"I'll be looking forward to hearing from you."

Seth pocketed the card and sat back down, patting Gomer on the head.

Across the porch, Chester called out, "Whatever that man just told you, you pay attention to it. One of the best damn men on the face of the planet."

Seth smiled at his dad. "You got it, Pops."

CHAPTER 16

*A*llison leaned back in bed. She had the television on, but it was muted. Loretta was asleep again. Zeke had said she was malnourished, and because she was run down, she'd been susceptible to infection, both viral and bacterial. He'd recommended sleep and food and to call him if she developed a fever. Loretta's shivering had stopped, and Zeke had thought it might have been caused by stress.

Allison watched the muted news program without really seeing it. For a Sunday, today had been … well, it had started wonderful, bumped into shocking, and ended with exhaustion. Her phone vibrated on the bedside stand. She grabbed it, smiling at the picture of Seth she'd snapped this morning. He was gorgeous. "Hey. How's Chester tonight?"

Seth sighed, "He got confused tonight. Wanted to know where Mom was."

"Oh, Seth." She wished she could be there to hold him.

"It's okay. Just hard not knowing what to say. The doctor told me not to argue with him because she's still alive in his mind."

"What did you tell him?"

"She was in town, and I didn't know when she'd be back. That settled him." He sighed. "What did the doctor say about your house guest?"

"Loretta," Allison said. "Well, I learned a lot just listening. She goes by Lottie, and she's twenty-three. She doesn't have insurance and refused to give her last name." Allison glanced at the shut door and lowered her voice even further as she continued to talk. "She's dehydrated, starving, and exhausted. Zeke thinks she'll get better with food and rest. I'm positive someone has beaten her, and so is Stephanie. That's Zeke's wife, Declan Howard's sister."

"Wait, she didn't marry Andrew Hollister?"

"Nope. Another long story I'll catch you up on

later, but Andrew is married to Gen, who owns the diner in town."

"Wow. Okay, but back on topic. Do you still want me to come in tomorrow and talk to her?"

Allison closed her eyes. "I do. I want to make sure she's safe. I don't know who hurt her, but someone has. I hate it. They have to be stopped and, if possible, punished for what they've done."

"I agree." Seth's voice lowered. "I wanted to give you the choice, though. I'll be as gentle as I can be with her, although it would be better if Ken interviewed her."

"I know. I just don't know if she'd talk." Allison turned off the television and slid down in bed.

"I talked to Frank Marshall today while the doctor and his wife were with you," Seth said after a moment.

Allison's eyes popped open. "You did? What did he want?"

"To offer me a job. I can't say much more than that." Seth hedged like all the people who worked at the Marshall ranch. She was used to that type of avoidance and knew exactly what it meant. Or thought she did.

"And? Are you going to take it?" It would mean

he'd be permanent here. Her breath stopped as she waited for him to answer.

"At first, no. I turned him down," Seth said. "I told him I can't leave Dad during the day. He needs someone with him all the time. It's not safe otherwise."

"At first?" Her hopes rose a bit. "What do you mean at first?"

"Mr. Marshall said the county could get someone in during the week. A nurse paid through Dad's insurance and Medicare."

She sat back up in bed. "That's good, right?"

"Yeah, but …" He sighed. "I don't understand it, but it feels like I'd be letting him down and, if I'm honest, like I'm handing him off. Letting someone do the hard part. That doesn't sit well in my gut."

"Seth, you've been doing the hard part. Every single day. You get up early, manage his meds, clear up his confusion, make sure he eats, and make sure he's safe. You're doing the job of an entire team of people."

"It's what he needs." Seth sighed.

"I agree," she murmured. "But what do *you* need?"

Seth was quiet for a long time. She could hear him breathing, so she knew the connection was still there. She wasn't going to push him. She'd let him think as long as he needed to do so.

"What do you think?" he finally asked.

"Honest?" She needed to know if she should say what she'd been thinking.

"That's what we do, right? Complete honesty?"

"It is. Okay, well ... The way I see it, you've already sacrificed a lot. You've put your career on hold. You've given up your freedom to care for your dad, which not many would do these days. And now, someone is offering you a way to keep helping your dad and reclaim part of who you are. That's not handing him off; that's balance."

"And if something happens when I'm not there?"

Allison understood the guilt that was playing into his decision. "A nurse would be trained to handle it." She leaned forward a bit. "And you'd be a phone call away. And the idea that you have to take care of your dad alone isn't good for you, Seth. That's burnout waiting to happen. You have too much heart to let your dad's care fail. If you don't think the nurse could handle your dad, then that's one thing, but you won't know until you arrange a meeting and see them interact."

Seth was quiet again for a moment, but finally, he said. "I do miss working."

Allison smiled softly, even though he couldn't see it. "Then maybe it's time to let someone else carry part of the load, so you can do more than survive. It is okay to have a life during this time."

"I have you, which is more than I ever hoped for," Seth said, his voice low and gravelly.

"You do have me," Allison said. "I'm not going anywhere. We have time to figure out where we fit into everything. That isn't a question in my mind."

"I know where I want to be," Seth said.

"And where's that?"

"Anywhere you are," Seth said. "What's between us is real. I haven't had this type of intimacy, not just sexually, but this, what we're doing now. Talking. This is … special to me."

A tear rolled down her cheek. "Oh, Seth."

"Are you crying?" Concern rang through the connection.

She reassured him, "Yeah, but good tears."

"Why?"

She laughed softly. "You touched my soul with those words. This is special to me, too. You are special to me, and I feel like a teenager saying it after only six weeks."

"When it's right, what does it matter how many hours or days have ticked by?"

"Some would say we're doomed because there aren't that many hours or days between us."

"Then they don't know us, do they?"

She smiled. "No, they don't."

"It's late. Go to sleep, babe. I'll see you tomorrow."

"What are you going to do about your dad?" She slid back down under the covers.

"I'm going to see what assistance I can get and then decide. Someone I care for suggested that." She could hear the smile in his voice.

"Well, that person is pretty smart." Allison rolled her eyes.

"You are, but I don't think you give yourself enough credit for that. Good night. I'll see you tomorrow."

"Good night."

Allison disconnected the call, then put the phone on her bedside table and pulled the covers up, smiling at the ceiling. This, what was between them, was special, and he was right. People who may judge them didn't know them, and she wouldn't let her mind create problems that didn't exist. Lord knew there were enough real-world problems to go around.

CHAPTER 17

Seth took a slow breath and sat in the armchair across from the couch, where Loretta sat curled into herself, eyes fixed on the floor. She hadn't moved much since Allison had let him in. Not even when Gomer had nosed her hand and whined softly, sensing something broken in her. He'd brought Gomer with him for that exact reason, but the woman didn't reach out to the dog, which was unusual. Not unheard of but unusual. Allison's mom was watching Chester while he whittled with Delbert, without his knowledge, of course. Seth now had time to develop a sense of safety for the young woman. With Gomer lying on the rug, still and watchful, he talked to Allison as she got him a cup of coffee.

Outside the apartment window, Hollister moved through the rhythm of a quiet afternoon. The wind rustled across the eaves, an occasional engine from Main Street sounded, and distant laughter from kids leaving school drifted through the open windows. Safe. Ordinary. Hollister at its finest.

He leaned forward, resting his forearms on his knees. "Loretta," She flinched at the word.

"Lottie," she supplied. "Please. I don't like Loretta."

"Lottie. Are you from around here? The reason I ask is that we want to help you. We won't let anyone hurt you. We just need to know what's going on. Help us help you, okay?"

She didn't answer at first. Her fingers worked at the edge of the fabric on her knee, eyes locked on a patch of carpet near Gomer. "Spearfish." She barely breathed the word.

Seth leaned in, and Gomer's head popped up, his tongue lolling sideways out of his mouth. "I want to make sure I heard you. You said you're from Spearfish?"

She nodded, her hair falling forward, hiding half her face.

"How'd you end up here?"

She hesitated. Long enough he almost thought she wouldn't answer.

"I waited until he went to work," she said finally. "Took what I could carry. Got to the highway and just ... kept going."

The words were quiet. Measured. But her knuckles were white where she clutched the hem of Allison's hand-me-down hoodie.

"He?"

She nodded, and her eyes filled with tears.

"Who is he?"

She shook her head. "I can't tell you. He'll kill me."

Okay, he'd come at it from another direction. "That's fair. Can you tell me, did he cause the bruises? Was he hurting you?" Seth asked gently.

Her breath caught, and for a heartbeat, she didn't move. Then she gave a tiny nod, as if any more than that might shatter her.

Seth waited. Silence was a void that most people couldn't let sit. She didn't look at him as she said softly, "He, he ... I made him lose his temper."

Seth said nothing. Just let her fill the silence.

"I thought I could make it right. Thought if I was better, quieter ... he wouldn't ..." Her voice cracked. "But it got worse."

She looked up, her eyes red, brimming but determined. "I didn't think he'd stop that night. He finally got tired and went to bed. I waited till morning and left before he got home from work."

Seth's jaw clenched. He'd seen bruises on soldiers, civilians, and kids in war zones. But this? This was worse. The damage ran deep, past the skin, past the fear. Into her spirit.

She kept going, barely above a whisper. "I hitched rides. A couple of decent folks. Then a couple who … weren't. They gave me the creeps. Kept asking weird questions. I told them I needed to use the bathroom, and I ran when we stopped here in Hollister. Hid behind the dumpsters at the gas station until they left. My bag was still in their back seat."

"All your stuff?" Seth asked.

"A little money. My phone. My ID." Her fingers twisted in the fabric at her knees. "Everything."

Seth swore silently. Outside, he was controlled and quiet. This woman didn't need to see any anger. She'd seen enough from the bastard who'd beat her.

"I thought I saw his truck on the highway," she added. "Far behind us once. It didn't turn into Hollister, but … it felt like he was close. Watching. It still does."

A single tear slipped down her cheek. She didn't brush it away as she continued, "I was going to ask if someone had day work, maybe wash dishes, sweep floors, anything. But I saw his truck come back and turn into town. He was *here*. He went into the diner and the gas station. I scurried under the boardwalk and hid. He stood over me." Tears flowed down her face. "He tried to get into both of the shops. He was so mad. I could hear him."

"You ended up sleeping under the boardwalk instead."

Her head dipped. "Yeah."

Seth ran a hand down his jaw. "You didn't do anything wrong. You know that, right?" She shrugged. He leaned forward but not too much because she was still terrified. He kept his voice steady. "You survived. You got out. That takes guts, Lottie."

She met his eyes but only for a second. Her voice was raw when she said, "I'm scared he'll hurt someone else just to punish me. I was trying to get to my aunt in North Dakota. She's the only one who ever helped me. She'd take me in, but if he thinks I went to her..."

"My question is, how did he know you were

here?" Seth said out loud. "But that isn't an issue anymore. You're safe here. That's a promise."

She looked at him then, really looked. There was so much fear in her eyes. "I don't want anyone to get hurt because of me."

"They won't. You're not alone in this anymore." He stood, letting the weight of his words settle between them.

"I'm going to talk to Ken. He's the county sheriff. We need to get this on record. We'll figure it out."

"The police won't help."

Seth stopped. "Why do you say that?"

"Because they didn't believe the neighbors. They called it in when they heard him hitting me. He made me tell them I'd fallen, that I was okay, that nothing was wrong. When they left, he threatened the lady next door. He told her he'd beat me to death if she called again." She sniffed and wiped at her nose. "They never came back."

"We can't be intimidated, Lottie," Allison said from where she stood. "If anyone tried that here, they'd find out what small town justice looked like and fast."

Seth nodded. "If he shows up, he'll have to get through us and every citizen of this town."

Loretta glanced from Allison to him slowly, her

face pale but a little less hollow. Maybe, just maybe, she'd started to believe them.

"What's your aunt's name? We can make sure she's okay."

"You'd do that?" Lottie's eyes held a glimmer of hope.

"Yes," Seth said. Even if he had to drive to North Dakota to make sure it happened. She gave him the information. Seth vowed he'd do everything in his power to make sure her past never touched her future again. He stood up and noticed how Lottie involuntarily flinched as he did. He put his hand on Allison's shoulder and said, "I'm going to step out and call Ken."

Allison smiled and covered his hand with hers for a moment. That connection was just what he needed. She was his grounding point, and that was a revelation.

Seth stepped out onto the back stairs of the building, letting the screen door thud shut behind him. The cold crept under his collar, but he welcomed it. Needed it. The air was sharp with dust and pine, the faint scent of cows drifting from the stockyard just out of town.

He hit Ken's number, which was now on speed

dial, and pressed the phone to his ear. The sheriff answered on the third ring.

"Zorn."

"It's Seth."

"What's up?"

"I've got a situation."

A pause. "Chester?"

"No. Remember that girl Allison called you about?"

"Yeah. No one ever saw her, though."

Seth glanced back through the glass. He could just see Loretta through the kitchen window, hunched on a stool, holding a mug between both hands like it was the only warm thing in the world.

"She's sitting in Allison's kitchen. Early twenties. Showed up dirty, scared, and half-starved. Allison called the doctor to check her out yesterday. The girl was terrified and refused to talk and demanded no police. I talked to her today and got some answers."

"Name?"

"Loretta. Goes by Lottie. Says she's from Spearfish. She's running from someone who beat her so bad she should've been in a hospital. Didn't file a report, didn't go to the ER. Just waited until he went to work, grabbed what she could, and left."

Ken blew out a breath. "Goddamn."

"She's scared he'll go after her aunt in North Dakota. She doesn't want to contact anyone in case he's tracking her."

"Is he?"

Seth rubbed the back of his neck. "Yeah, he is. Question is how. She said she thought he was following her and the couple that had picked her up hitchhiking, but the truck passed Hollister. He came back soon after. She dove under the boardwalk and watched him. She said he went to the diner, the gas station, and then tried to get into the bakery and the clothes shop next door. Both were closed then, so it had to be after two."

Another long pause. "Yeah, Kayla was gone for a couple of weeks. That makes sense. She tell you his name?" Ken asked.

"No," Seth said. "Not yet. I'm not pushing her right now. She's on the edge. Thought she was going to bolt when I asked her where she's from."

"Shit."

"Yeah."

Ken was quiet again. When he spoke, his voice had settled into that low, steady tone Seth recognized.

"You trust her?"

"I trust the bruises under her sleeves and how she

watches every door. I trust that she's got more fear than guile."

"All right. I'll run what I can from this end quietly. I'll cross-reference missing persons and domestic disturbances in the area. If he's got a history, I'll find it."

"Appreciate it."

"You armed?" Ken asked.

Seth's mouth twitched. "Rifle in the truck, dog at my side. No one is going to fuck with us."

"You think he'll come here?"

"I think if he's got half a brain, he won't. But if he's the kind of man who puts his fists on a woman and still thinks he owns her, then yeah. He might show up again. That's why Lottie kept hidden and ate out of garbage cans."

"I'll have the deputy run some extra passes past the bakery. Night and morning."

"Keep it subtle. She's skittish, and if even a fraction of what she's saying is true, he's not stupid." Seth paused. "I have the aunt's name." He provided it to Ken.

"You call if anything changes," Ken said. "See if you can get a description of the truck or this asshole's name."

"Will do."

Seth ended the call and lowered the phone, staring out over the alley and rooftops. The town looked peaceful.

It always did.

He turned back toward the door, already making a mental list of the questions he would ask. He glanced at the window and saw Lottie talking to Allison. He'd let them talk for a couple of minutes before going back in. That young woman had run through hell and landed in Hollister. He wasn't about to let the devil find her. Speaking of which, he walked down the stairs and around the building. Sure enough, there was a divot in the dirt. He stretched under the boardwalk and pulled the clothes she was using as bedding out of the dirt.

CHAPTER 18

The smell of warm bread and cinnamon still clung to the walls upstairs, even though the ovens downstairs had been off for hours. Outside the apartment window, October had turned crisp and cold.

Allison shut the windows that had been open that afternoon and stirred honey into two mugs of chamomile tea. She carried them to the small table tucked beneath the window. Lottie sat there, knees drawn up, staring out over Main Street like she expected something awful to appear around the corner at any second.

"Here," Allison said gently, setting the mug in front of her. "Drink. You've got to be running on empty."

Lottie took it with both hands, fingers trembling around the ceramic. She didn't sip, just held the warmth close like it might keep her together.

"I don't know why I asked for help," she murmured.

"Because you weren't going to make it if you didn't," Allison said, sitting across from her. "You needed the strength to survive, and you found it." Allison watched her carefully. "You want to talk about it?"

Another long pause. Then Lottie nodded. Once. Barely.

"It started so small," she said. "Little things. He didn't like my friends. Said they were jealous of what we had. Toxic. That's what he called them. Told me I didn't need them." Her eyes didn't lift from the mug. "Then he didn't like my job. Said my boss flirted with me. He asked me if I encouraged my boss. I didn't, I swear."

The desperation in her voice almost killed her. Allison blinked. "I believe you."

Lottie drew a shaky breath. "He made me feel disgusting for going to work so my boss could flirt. He made me stop wearing makeup. If I laughed at anyone else's jokes, he'd say I was into them or wanted them more than I wanted him."

Allison's chest tightened. She didn't interrupt. Just let the girl speak.

"I quit. He said he'd take care of me. That's what he always said. *I'll take care of you.* And I believed him." Lottie's lip trembled. "God help me, I believed him."

"You didn't do anything wrong," Allison said softly.

Lottie shook her head, fast and sharp. "No. That's the thing. I *did*. Everything was my fault. If he was angry, it was because I made him that way. I didn't mean to do it, but I always did. If he hit something, it was because I provoked him. He would get mad if I flinched, but I couldn't stop." Her voice broke. "He hurt me."

Allison reached across the table and gently covered Lottie's knee. The girl didn't pull away.

"The last time," Lottie whispered, "he knocked me into the kitchen counter so hard I split my eyebrow open. I remember staring at the blood on the tile, wondering if I'd get to clean it before he made me explain it."

Allison's gut twisted. The bastard. "He made you explain why you were bleeding?"

"Yeah. I had to explain how I messed up. What I did to make him so mad."

Allison sat back. "That's insane."

Lottie looked at her. "He said if I ever left him or if I ever embarrassed him in front of anyone, he'd kill me. And I believe him, Allison. I really do. If he finds me, he'll kill me. He won't yell. He won't drag me home. He'll just end it. He's told me how. He will choke me. Face-to-face so he can watch me die."

Allison felt her heart twist. There was no exaggeration in Lottie's voice. No drama. Just the clear, simple certainty of someone who'd lived in survival mode for too long.

"Well," she said firmly, "he's not going to find you. Not here. Not in *my* town."

Lottie blinked, surprised by the strength in Allison's tone.

"Hollister may be small," Allison went on, "but it's tight knit. People notice strangers. They care. They ask questions. The folks here? They'd move heaven and earth to protect someone in need. Especially from someone who thinks raising his fists against a woman makes him a man."

Lottie's lip quivered. "But I'm not from here."

"That doesn't matter," Allison said. "You're here now. And no one hurts people in Hollister and walks away without the whole damn town standing in their path."

Silence stretched between them, broken only by the tick of the wall clock and the faint sounds of the wind in the trees outside.

Lottie finally took a sip of tea, her hands steadying just a little. "Thank you," she whispered. "For seeing me."

"You don't have to thank me, sweetheart." Allison gave her hand a gentle squeeze. "You're safe. We've got you. No one's going to let him touch you again."

* * *

The clothes were damp and stiff with cold. Bundled together were crusted fleece and a thrift store windbreaker. They smelled of old wood, earth, and weeks without washing. Seth stood there for a beat, crouched in the shadows beneath the slats, the late afternoon wind dragging dust across gravel behind him.

That's when he saw it, buried inside a pocket.

A dead Apple Watch.

Black band, cracked face, silent.

He swore under his breath and shoved it in his coat pocket before striding back up the embankment toward the bakery.

He found Lottie sitting on the floor in the living

room, legs folded under her, a blanket wrapped around her shoulders. She looked up when he came in. Her eyes were puffy and red but clear.

"Hey," she said quietly.

Seth didn't answer right away. He crossed to the table and set the bundle of clothes down gently. Then he pulled the watch from his pocket and held it up. "This was in your jacket."

Her brow furrowed, then she smiled faintly. "My watch. I forgot it was even in there."

"It's dead," he said. "But it could have been broadcasting your location when it was charged."

The words landed like stones.

Lottie stared at the device, her face going pale. "No…"

"He could have followed it. Not directly to here, but close. Close enough to find you if he were looking."

Her whole body recoiled. The blanket slipped from her shoulders as she stood too fast, stumbling back toward the wall like she'd been struck.

"Oh, God."

"He's not here," Seth said calmly. "But this? I bet my next paycheck that this was his beacon, Lottie. One you didn't even know you were carrying."

She looked at the watch, then at Seth, and her voice broke. "I thought I was free."

"You are," he said, stepping forward, his voice gentler now. "I'm not plugging it in. No one is. It's done."

She wrapped her arms around her middle and sank onto the edge of the couch. "I'm so stupid. How could I not know? I was carrying it the whole time."

"You weren't stupid," Seth said firmly. "You were surviving. And he counted on that. It's what predators like him do. Bank on you not knowing, not asking. That's how men like him keep control. But it's over now."

She shook her head, tears spilling silently. "He'll come. If he thinks I'm alive. If he thinks I'm out here … He'll find me. He said he'd kill me if I ever made him look weak. If I embarrassed him."

Seth knelt in front of her, resting one steady hand on the couch cushion near hers.

"We've already got the sheriff looped in. With your permission, we'll let the rest of the town know. Quietly. Folks around here don't take kindly to men who hurt women. They'll keep their eyes open. He won't get far."

Lottie hesitated, her voice barely audible. "What will they think of me?"

"They won't even wonder. This is Hollister. People watch out for each other. You're one of us now."

She nodded slowly, then again, more sure. "Okay. Tell them. Please."

Seth reached for his phone but paused. "Lottie ... I need his name. And a description."

She swallowed hard. "Eric Danvers. He's twenty-eight. Six-foot-one. Stocky. Blond buzz cut. Has a scar on his chin and a burn mark on his left hand. He got it when he threw a pan at me, and the grease spilled on his hand."

Seth didn't react, but his gut twisted.

"He drives a navy-blue Chevy Silverado. Extended cab. Big dent on the passenger side from when he got drunk and ran into a mailbox. He keeps saying he'll fix it, but he never does."

"Plates?"

She shook her head. "I don't remember. It's a South Dakota plate, but I only saw it once. He always parked in the garage. I wasn't allowed in there."

Seth nodded, already committing every word to memory.

She gripped the edge of the cushion, knuckles white. "Seth ... if he comes, don't try to talk to him. He'll twist everything I said around. He'll make you believe him." Tears brimmed over her bottom lashes.

"I won't."

She was shaking, "Promise me."

"I promise." His voice was low, hard. "If Eric Danvers sets one foot in Hollister, I'll make sure he wishes he hadn't."

She exhaled shakily, her shoulders trembling, then leaned forward until her forehead pressed against her knees.

Seth stood and stepped into the hallway, and wrapped his arm around Allison, who had tears in her eyes, too. His jaw clenched, phone already dialing.

This was no longer just protection.

It was war.

Ken answered on the first ring.

"You've got something?"

Seth stood in the hallway and spoke so both women could hear him.

"I found out how he was tracking her."

Ken didn't speak, just waited.

"She had a smart watch in her jacket. It was dead when I found it, but he could've followed her here if he'd been using an app or paired account. It wouldn't be exact like a military grade GPS, but it would have kept him close, at least. Maybe that's why he drove past and then circled back."

"Damn it. That makes sense," Ken muttered. "She know?"

"Now she does." Seth's jaw tightened. "She freaked out when I told her he could've been tracking her with the watch. She thought she was being careful."

"She was," Ken said flatly. "He was just being a snake."

"That's what I told her, too." There was silence again, both men chewing on what that meant.

"She gave permission for the town to be notified. Quietly. I've got a name and a vehicle."

"Go," Ken said.

"Eric Danvers. Twenty-eight. From Spearfish. Six-foot-one, stocky, blond buzz cut, scar on his chin, burn scar on his left hand. Drives a navy-blue Chevy Silverado, extended cab. The passenger side's dented bad from a drunk driving incident she witnessed."

"Plates?"

"South Dakota. No number. Always parked backed in. Hiding it."

"Figures. I can find out with this information."

"I told her we'd protect her," Seth said, voice low. "And I meant it."

"So do I," Ken said. "Listen, I'll call in my deputy. He can start spreading the word to folks we trust. Old guard, ranch hands, business owners. People who'll keep their mouths shut and their eyes open."

"Start with Edna," Seth said. "She sees everything, and nobody questions her when she talks."

Ken snorted. "You think I wasn't already headed there?"

Seth didn't smile.

"He shows his face here, we shut it down fast," Ken said, voice hardening. "This town doesn't have a lot of rules, but we don't take kindly to men like that thinking they can pick up where they left off."

"He threatened to kill her, and she has no doubt he'll do it."

Ken exhaled slowly, tightly. "Then he doesn't get the benefit of the doubt."

"She's terrified he'll go after her aunt in North Dakota. If he knows she's not with her, that might be the only thing keeping her aunt safe."

"I contacted North Dakota law enforcement. They've got eyes up there. Discreet."

"Good."

"I want that watch," Ken added. "Just in case we can pull anything from it."

"I'll bring it to you. I have to get Dad anyway."

"Hey, Seth?"

"Yeah?"

"Be ready. Make sure Allison knows what to do," Ken said. "He might already be close."

Seth ended the call without another word. Gomer stood near the back step, muscles tight, ears perked, watching the shadows at the far end of the alley.

Seth looked out the picture window in Allison's apartment. There was nothing but a few parked trucks, closed shop windows, and the slow flicker of a porchlight turning on in the distance. The fucker might be close, which would put Allison in danger. He held onto Allison as he made another call.

"Hello?"

"Sarah, I need your help."

"What do you need? Is Dad okay?"

"He's the same. We have a situation here, and I need to be free to handle it."

"Talk to me," Sarah said, and Seth laid it out for her.

"Okay. I'll make some calls. Gramma and Grandpa Miles should be okay with watching the girls for a week or two if you need me to stay longer. I have to put things in order. I'll be there tomorrow night."

"I wouldn't ask if I didn't think it was important."

"Don't you dare apologize. He is a cranky old fart, but I love him, and I told you we'd share the responsibility of taking care of him." Sarah huffed. "I'll see you late afternoon or early evening tomorrow. Do I need to bring anything?"

"A pillow and some linens, and blankets for your bed." He hadn't gotten around to ordering anything for the other rooms. He and Chester were set, though.

Sarah chuckled. "I can do that. I haven't slept in a twin bed in years. I'll see you soon." The line went dead.

Seth glanced down at Allison. "Sarah's coming so I can focus on you and Lottie."

"I'd feel better if you were here with us at night."

"Starting tomorrow night, I will be." He wanted that fucker. It was the most basic feeling. If anything happened to Allison, he'd fucking go insane. What they had was new, but it was something he'd kill to protect. Feral didn't come close to the primal sensations that flowed through him. He would protect Allison. He wouldn't fail.

CHAPTER 19

Seven motherfucking weeks since he'd come home to find her gone. Seven weeks of rage at the audacity of the fucking little bitch. Eric had let that rage settle into a specific plan of action. He had been tracking that slut with her watch, but it went dead right here. In Hollister. The bitch had probably let it run out of power. But he figured she'd charge it back up. She hadn't. So, he did what he thought she would do. He went to her aunt's in North Dakota. That was a waste of time.

He'd taken as much vacation from work as he could. Then that bitch made him quit a good paying job to find her. Whatever. He'd find her, and she'd pay. His knuckles cracked as he gripped the steering wheel. For over two weeks, he'd parked down the block from her aunt's house in Fargo. Two weeks of watching the front porch, the back alley, and the curtains at night. Nothing. Not a shadow. Not a whisper of her.

He'd waited. He'd followed deliveries. He meticulously tracked her aunt to church, the grocery, and even a hair appointment.

Loretta never showed.

Which meant she'd *lied*.

Which meant she knew exactly what she was doing when she ran. She'd had a plan, and she was laughing at him now. Laughing because she'd played him.

His jaw flexed, slow and tight. His hand curled into a fist on the worn leather of the steering wheel.

He couldn't forgive her for making him look like a fool. No. That had to be corrected.

The truck engine ticked as it cooled, the only sound in the otherwise dead parking lot of the Bit and Spur. No cars. No lights. The bar was closed. It was too early even for the drunks and the drifters, and that was why he liked it. The parking lot was roped off, and the building was decorated. Obviously, a big party was happening soon. What the fuck ever. He would be gone as soon as he found her.

Eric sat behind the wheel of the Silverado,

watching the sleepy town of Hollister across the highway like a hunter waiting for a twitch in the grass.

So small. So smug. The little Main Street was lit by a string of old-fashioned lamps, one or two flickering yellow against the lingering darkness. A bakery light glowed like a beacon down the street. He'd been there before. He stared at it the longest. Her watch had pinpointed that building. But the business was closed. It closed at two, and when he was there, it was two-thirty.

Loretta was there. He could feel it. He'd followed the trail of her smart watch. He'd enabled that tracker on the watch before giving it to her.

Eric smiled coldly. The last ping from her watch was smack dab in the middle of this town. It might not have been the bakery, but she was close. He knew it. Then it went dark. But not before it gave him a place to come back to, after he returned to the house and gathered a few things. He even went back to North Dakota, not believing the bitch was smart enough to go somewhere else. But once again, he couldn't find her. He'd even broken into the fucking house when the aunt had left for church. Nothing. No clothes, no extra things that indicated another person was in the house. He'd left a message, though.

He'd trashed that house and taken out his anger on every possession that old woman had. It had been therapeutic and dulled his rage. That was how he'd devised the plan of watching the sleepy little town. She wouldn't say shit. She knew he'd kill her if she did. So, he only needed to wait, watch, and be invisible.

He reached for the coffee he'd bought an hour ago from the diner and took a slow sip. It was damn good, but taste didn't matter. What mattered was that Hollister felt … soft.

Too few buildings. Too many open spaces. These were the kinds of places where people left doors unlocked and assumed their secrets were safe. He could already picture it. The look on her face when she saw him again. Shock, then maybe terror. Oh, then … yeah, then that empty look of resignation she always gave him when she knew she'd gone too far.

He missed that look. It was his favorite. The one he loved the most. Just before the first strike. That was the best. He craved that look and that feeling of his fist against her body. The rest of the blows didn't give him that high, but her small cries got him to the point where he could stop and go jack off. She always got him to that point. Others hadn't.

And the bitch thought she'd gotten away. He'd

taught her better than that. She would leave him when she was dead. Not before.

Eric's eyes flicked to the rearview mirror, scanning the empty lot again. He hadn't parked facing the street. That was amateur stuff. Park at an angle where his plate couldn't be seen from the highway. He wasn't stupid.

He'd give this town more time. Just watch. Map out the comings and goings. Who went where? What businesses opened early? What buildings had upstairs windows? There weren't many.

Then he'd move. He'd start at the building where he lost her signal. And locked doors wouldn't stop him this time.

* * *

THE BAKERY SMELLED like yeast and butter and fall seasonings. Allison had just pulled the first tray of pumpkin coffee cake from the oven when the bell above the front door jingled. She frowned. It was too early for her regular customers. She frowned, wiping her hands on her apron as she crossed into the front room.

"Edna?"

The older woman didn't smile. Her winter coat

was unzipped, lipstick smudged a bit, so she'd probably been at the diner having her caramel roll. Her wispy gray hair frizzed around her ears from the brisk wind outside.

"Morning, sweetheart," she said, voice low. "You got a minute?"

Allison nodded. "Hi, yourself. What brings you by so early? Come on back. Coffee's fresh."

Edna followed her behind the counter into the kitchen, her boots tapping sharply on the tile. She didn't sit. Just stood there, her eyes flicking toward the stairwell that led to the apartment upstairs.

"She still up there?" she asked quietly.

Allison nodded. Everyone knew where Lottie was staying. The news had spread like wildfire as soon as Ken had told Edna. The people of Hollister now did a double-take at everything and everyone. "She is. I haven't heard her, so she's still sleeping, I think."

Edna exhaled through her nose, then leaned in. "I saw a truck this morning. I was heading into the diner. Took the long way because it's my morning to have a caramel roll with Kate. Need to burn some calories."

Allison's stomach dropped. "What kind of truck?"

"Dark blue Chevy. Extended cab. Dent on the

passenger side big as a sin. Parked outside the diner before sunup."

Allison gripped the edge of the counter. "Did you see the driver?"

Edna nodded slowly. "Didn't recognize him. Not local. Stocky fella, military haircut. Face looked tight. Mean. Like someone who hadn't smiled in a long time and didn't plan to."

"Did he talk to anyone?"

"Nope, not that I saw. I came in just after him. He got a coffee to go from Corrie. Didn't make eye contact. Left fast. But he looked around like he was checking every corner of this town. Like he was mapping it in his head."

Allison swallowed hard. "He see you watching him?"

Edna gave her a sharp look. "Honey, I've been blending into diner booths since before you were in training bras. He didn't give me a second glance."

The tremble Allison had been holding at bay settled in her hands. She turned toward the coffee pot, pouring herself a mug so Edna wouldn't see her face.

"Damn, what do I do now? What do I tell her?" she asked, her voice barely above a whisper.

Edna's hand came to rest gently on her back.

"You keep your chin up. You keep that girl safe. And you let the rest of us do what we do best."

Allison turned.

"And what's that?"

Edna's eyes narrowed. "We notice everything. We talk. And when danger rolls into town wearing a dented truck and a bad attitude, Hollister circles the wagons."

Allison reached for her phone. "Ken knows?"

"I called him before I came. He's already moving. Seth, too, I imagine. Although he has Chester to care for."

Allison shook her head. "No, Sarah, his sister came in last night. Seth called her when Lottie told us what had happened. He wanted to be able to move without worrying about his dad. She's staying for a week but can extend it to two weeks if …" Allison swallowed the knot rising in her throat. "Can you watch the shop? I'm going to run up and tell Seth."

Edna leaned in, voice like gravel and steel. "You got it. This asshole picked the wrong damn town."

CHAPTER 20

Seth settled into a booth at the diner. One with an unobstructed view of the street and the bakery. He jerked his eyes to the door when the bell rang. As he recognized who'd come in, he blinked and then smiled. "Gregg?"

Gregg Koehler frowned and looked over. "Well, I'll be. What the hell are you doing back here?" Gregg walked over, and Seth stood up, shaking his old friend's hand.

"Came back to take care of my pops. Sit with me?"

"I can do that." Gregg sat down, and Corrie came out. "Hi, Gregg, the usual?"

"Yes, please, ma'am," Gregg said and took off his cowboy hat. "You done with the military?"

"Yep. Retired. You?"

"I work for Mr. Marshall as a ranch hand."

"Not with your dad anymore?" Seth asked as he took a sip of his coffee.

"My dad killed my mom and fucked us up, bad. He's dead. The old ranch was plowed under. Good riddance."

"Holy hell." Seth set his coffee cup down. "I'm so damn sorry, dude. I knew things were bad out there …"

Gregg shrugged. "Bastard mentally and physically abused all of us. Christian the most. He escaped. Married. Has a son."

"Really?" Seth cocked his head.

"Yeah." Gregg looked him in the eye. "His husband is a good man. I don't tolerate anyone saying anything about either of them."

Seth smiled at his friend. "I wouldn't. Not my place nor my business."

"What are you doing here? Your pops okay?" he asked after Corrie put a platter-sized caramel roll and a coffee before him.

"Sarah is with him right now. I'm keeping an eye out for a certain truck."

Gregg stopped with his coffee halfway to his lips. "Been briefed. Seen it?"

"Edna did yesterday morning. Deputies are keeping it casual, but we haven't seen it again. Everyone is watching."

"I'm off today. Come in on my off days for this." He nodded to his plate. "I could stay if you're needing help."

"I wouldn't mind the company." Seth leaned back in the booth. "You realize you'll have to tell me the whole story, right? About your mom. I thought she left."

"You always were a nosy son of a bitch," Gregg said before shoving a forkful of caramel roll into his mouth.

"That's what friends are good at."

Gregg huffed and asked around his food. "You staying?"

"Yeah. Allison and I have the start of something special. Dad is going to need care for quite a while. Or at least I'm hoping he will. Alzheimer's."

Gregg nodded. "Knew that. You going to take that job at the ranch?"

Seth cocked his head. "How did you know about that?"

"Ranch manager said Mr. Marshall had words with you. Figured you must have a military skill he needs." Gregg looked at him. "And I didn't say that."

"Best kept non-secret in town."

Gregg pointed his fork at Seth. "That," he said.

"Start talking, Koehler," Seth said as he poured another cup of coffee from the carafe that Corrie had brought out.

Gregg sighed and leaned back. "Well, Christian and I are the only ones left."

"What? What happened to Clint?"

"Turns out he was a serial killer," Gregg said, shrugging.

Seth blinked. "You're shitting me."

Gregg shook his head and looked around the diner. "What do you say we wait for this conversation until after I finish? We can stroll around town, look for that truck, and I can fill you in on all of it."

"Deal." Seth took a sip of his coffee. My God, Hollister wasn't short on drama, was it?

THE STREETS of Hollister were wrapped in dusk, the kind that stretched long across the prairies. The purple light bleeding into deep shadow. The bakery had closed hours ago, but Allison's light still glowed above the back door. Seth's gut had been twisting all day. That weight he got before everything went sideways. He, Gregg, and Gomer had walked the town all day. That damn truck wasn't in sight. Still, he couldn't shake the feeling of dread.

"Did you hear that?" he asked Gregg. Gomer's ears were pinned forward, and he growled low in his chest. "Come on." He and Gregg started jogging toward the back of the bakery.

He turned the corner just in time to hear Allison scream, "Let me go!"

He sprinted forward, Gomer at his side, Gregg just behind him. The road behind the bakery stretched out dark and narrow. Halfway down, he saw Allison struggling as she was dragged toward a truck.

And the man dragging her?

It had to be that motherfucker. Eric Danvers.

Big, blocky build. Blond hair with rage pouring off him like smoke off a fire.

Then Seth saw Lottie crumpled on the ground near the rear door. Unmoving.

His vision tunneled. "Gregg, get the women!"

Eric dropped Allison at the sound of his voice. She stumbled back, breath ragged, and Gregg swept in, grabbing her and pulling her to safety.

Seth didn't slow down.

He slammed into Eric with the full force of his

weight, both of them crashing hard against the side of the truck.

Eric snarled, "She's mine!"

Seth punched him. Once. Twice. Eric took the hits and answered with a fist to Seth's ribs, then a wild swing that split Seth's lip. They grappled, each looking for an advantage. Fists flew when separation happened. Seth's boots slipped against the gravel, but he didn't back up, and neither did that fucker Danvers.

Eric drove a shoulder into Seth's gut, slamming him into the trash cans. The edge caught Seth's back hard, and he grunted and twisted sharply, elbowing Eric in the temple. Eric staggered, eyes wild. "You think you can take her from me?" he panted. "You don't know what she is."

"I know what *you* are," Seth growled. "A coward who hits women."

Eric roared, pulling a folding knife from his back pocket and flicking it open. Seth barely dodged the first swipe.

"Gregg!" he barked, never taking his eyes off the blade.

"I've got them!" Gregg shouted from the back of the bakery. "Both are breathing!"

The knife flashed again. Eric slashed across Seth's

forearm, cutting deep. Pain flared, hot and bright, but Seth didn't stop. He stepped in fast, inside the blade, grabbed Eric's wrist, twisted until bones popped, and slammed his wrist against the blue truck. The knife clattered to the pavement.

Seth kneed the man and lost his balance as Eric swung at the same time. Eric staggered, disoriented, reaching blindly for the truck door with his good hand. Seth grabbed the back of his coat and spun the man down hard onto the gravel. Eric's head landed with a sickening thud, groaning, one arm twisted beneath him.

Sirens wailed in the distance. Then the headlights. Seth dropped his knees to Danvers' back and twisted both arms behind the man. He pushed them toward the man's neck, and Danvers roared, spittle flying as he screamed, "I'll kill her! I'm going to kill her!"

Ken's voice broke through Danvers' screaming, shouting orders.

"Step out, Seth!"

Seth obeyed, chest heaving, blood dripping from his arm. Gomer stood beside him, growling low, unmoving.

Ken and two deputies rushed in, guns drawn.

Ken knelt beside Eric, yanked his good arm back, and cuffed him hard.

"Eric Danvers, you're under arrest for attempted murder, aggravated assault, and attempted kidnapping. You have the right to remain silent."

Eric spat blood. "She's mine. I own that bitch, I'm going to kill her. You can't stop me."

Ken slammed the door on that with a knee drop onto his back.

"You'll do your talking in court."

Doc Johnson rushed past them to check on Lottie, who was having problems breathing.

Gregg held her as Doc Johnson examined her. Seth turned to look for Allison, who was upright, tear-streaked, and shaking. She found his gaze and didn't look away.

She got up and made her way to him, and they clung to each other until she pulled away. "I knew you'd come."

"I can't believe he got through to the bakery."

"I came out, and he was pulling in from that direction." Allison pointed out toward the darkness and the prairie behind. "When we started arguing, Lottie came outside. He raced up the stairs and pulled her down by her hair. She froze. She couldn't move. I saw the terror in her eyes. He grabbed her by the neck and squeezed. That's why I hit him with the trashcan cover. It got him off her, but ..."

"Onto you."

"It was worth it." She looked up at him. "I knew you'd come. I watched you fight him. I was afraid."

"For me?" he asked.

She shook her head. "No. I was afraid you'd kill him, and then Ken would have to arrest you."

Seth laughed and pulled her closer. "Gregg and I weren't far. You alerted us."

"Excuse me. I don't think we've met. I'm Dr. Johnson, and you, my friend, need some stitches."

Seth glanced at Allison. "Are you cut?"

"No, but you are," Zeke said, pointing to both lacerations.

"Oh, Seth." Allison bent over. "Oh, man."

"What's wrong?"

"Well, she hates the sight of her blood, but obviously, your bleeding affects her the same way."

Allison staggered and went down. Seth caught her and assisted her to the ground.

"Is she okay?"

"Yeah. Stephanie, my wife, will stay with her until she comes to. I need you and Lottie to come over to the clinic."

Seth wasn't about to leave her. Not a chance in hell. "I'll carry Allison."

"No, I'll carry her," Ken said. "You don't need to bleed anymore. You've already contaminated my crime scene."

"I am your fucking crime scene, asshole," Seth ground out.

"Yeah, I know," Ken said. Seth frowned at Ken as he bent down and picked Allison up. "Completely platonic, Seth. I have my woman. I don't want yours." Even so, the glare Seth flipped Ken was nothing less than territorial and lethal.

Doc Johnson dropped an arm on Ken's shoulder. "Come over for statements when you get done with this asshole, my man. Gregg, you got Lottie?"

"I do," Gregg said as he carefully cradled Lottie in his arms.

CHAPTER 21

Allison groaned as she woke up. She opened her eyes, blinking at the glaring lights above her. "Hey, you're back with us." Stephanie's voice turned her head.

"What?" She frowned and then bolted up. "Lottie? Seth?"

"Both are going to be fine. Zeke is stitching up Seth." Allison closed her eyes. "Oh, yeah."

"Figured you'd be better here than in there with him." Stephanie chuckled.

"Yeah, thanks." Allison sat up. "Ken has that bastard in custody, right?"

"Oh, yeah. Seth did a number on his wrist. But with Zeke so busy with Lottie, Seth, and you, he's waiting for the ambulance crew to come up from

Belle." Stephanie looked at her and smiled. "Sucks to be him."

"Right?" Allison smiled back at her, and then the expression dropped. "I saw him choking Lottie. I hit him with the lid of the garbage can to get him off her."

"How did he get behind the bakery?"

"Drove straight in from the back. We should probably tell the Hollisters to check their fencing." Allison rubbed the back of her neck. "Lottie came down to help me with wrapping the Fall Festival coffee cakes. She wouldn't be seen from the front. We were wrapping in the break room. Big mistake."

"You couldn't have known he was out in the field watching."

Allison shook her head. "She's okay?"

"She will be." Stephanie sighed. "It'll take a while for her to trust another human, that's for sure. Zeke wants to keep her with us overnight. Airway edema after strangulation could happen later, which would need intervention."

"I have some savings, Steph. I can pay for any care she receives."

Stephanie shook her head. "This is just time. Just a neighborly watch. Nothing to pay." Steph handed her a cup of water. "Feeling better?"

"Yeah. Thanks. I've never fainted at the sight of anyone else's blood before. Just mine." She frowned. "Weird."

"No, not really. You were in a high-stress situation, and it's pretty obvious you two are into each other."

"That's mild, but I'll admit to it." Allison chuckled.

"Well, I'm happy for you."

Allison smiled. "Thank you. Is Ken coming by for statements?"

"He's in with Lottie now. She's latched onto Gregg Koehler, though. He held her while the asshat was fighting Seth, so I think she's holding onto him as her safety net."

Allison took a sip of the water Steph had given her. "Wish this was a bit stronger."

"Sorry, the good stuff requires a prescription."

Allison opened her mouth to respond when the door opened, and Seth walked in. He lifted his arm. A pristine white bandage circled his arm. "No blood. Don't faint."

She made a face at him as he walked over and pulled her into his arms while she was sitting on the exam table. "God, that fight was the most vicious thing I've ever seen," Allison whispered.

Seth's arms tightened around her. "He didn't stand a chance until he pulled that knife. I'll give him credit. For a big guy, he was fast."

"For an insane asshat, you mean," Allison said and shivered at the memory of that knife. "Where did you learn how to fight like that?"

"Well, I'd like to say military training." Seth chuckled. "But in reality, I had a period of rebellion when I was a young airman and had a few bar fights. You learn fast to think on your feet. Thankfully, I was never caught." His hands rubbed up and down her back. "Zeke said I was good to go. Take me back to your place?"

She looked up at him. "Absolutely. Should we tell Lottie we're going?"

Seth nodded and bent down to kiss her lightly. "We'll do that."

Allison slid off the exam table, and Seth took her hand in his. Stephanie was in the hall when they walked out. "She's down there. Sorry, there was no way I couldn't hear you, and I was humming to myself as loud as I could."

Allison smiled at her friend. "No worries."

Seth knocked on the door and opened it. Ken looked around. "Ah, the warrior and the fainting princess."

"Ha, ha." Allison rolled her eyes at Ken and walked over to Lottie. "How are you?"

"I'm fine now. The doctor gave me something for anxiety." Lottie smiled. "You saved me. I heard you yelling before I lost consciousness."

"Yeah, he might have a bump on his head. I whapped him with the garbage can lid." Allison looked at Ken. "He must have been parked behind the bakery in Hollister's field."

"I'll get evidence of that in the morning and swing by to get your statements. Tracks and such can wait. It isn't supposed to rain for weeks." He glanced at Lottie's statement. "If you remember anything else, just give me a call."

"I will. Thank you," Lottie said. She glanced at Gregg and then down at their clasped hands. Lottie released her hold. "Thank you again, Gregg."

Gregg glanced at them and then nodded before he turned back to her. "I've been where you are. My father and my older brother were abusers. Physically and mentally tortured my other brother and me. Pitted us against each other. So, if you ever want to talk about things, I can listen. I can understand where you're at and what you're going through." He pointed to Seth and her. "They know everything and can tell you.

I'm safe." He nodded to Ken. "He's a dick, but he's safe, too."

Ken's mouth dropped open. "Well, thanks for the recommendation, Koehler."

Allison couldn't help the laughter that floated out of her. She needed to laugh after the night she'd had.

"Lottie, Stephanie said they want you to stay the night. I'll come over in the morning. You're free to stay with me."

"I don't want to impose." Lottie looked down.

"Mr. Marshall has a couple small cabins. Damn good locks, and the bastard wouldn't know where you were staying." Gregg glanced at his watch. "I can ask him tonight if you can use one until you get on your feet."

"I can't pay." She looked up at Gregg. Tears were forming in her eyes.

"You can if you work for me," Allison said. Could she afford an employee? Not really, but she'd make it work somehow.

"What?"

"Yeah. I'll teach you what I know, and you can help me out." She liked the idea more and more. "Plus, I bet Kayla could use help at her shop, too. Mom and Dad down at the general store are getting on in age and could use someone to help stock the lower shelves." She nodded and smiled. "Yeah, we can make this work."

"Why would you want to do that?"

"Because we can," Ken said. "I could use someone to clean the office once a week. We try to keep it up, but you know how guys are."

"Are you serious?" Lottie looked from one to the next.

"Absolutely. You don't worry about a thing. We'll talk more when you're feeling better." Allison smiled. "Right now, we're heading back to the apartment."

"And I need to make a run to the jail in Belle."

"There's a fresh pot of coffee over at the bakery. We were going to spend the night wrapping the Fall Festival goods."

"I'll stop by in a minute and fill my tankard. Thank you, Allison."

She smiled at Ken and, for the first time, didn't feel like she should apologize. "Not a problem." They said good night to Gregg, Zeke, and Stephanie, then walked back to the bakery. Her dad was sitting on the steps, and her mom was at the door when they turned the corner. "Stephanie said you were fine when I called, so I didn't come over." Her mom rushed over to her and hugged her. "The audacity of that monster to attack you and Lottie."

"Seth stopped him."

Seth shrugged. "I did what anyone would do."

Allison's dad crossed his arms. "Really?"

Seth smiled. "Well, anyone who thinks your daughter put the moon and sun in the heavens."

"And that is my cue," Ken said. "I'm going to grab some of that coffee, Allison. I don't need to fall asleep on the drive south."

"Oh, let me get it for you, Ken," her mom said and looked back at Allison. "I'm not going to sleep for the next week, so your dad and I will package the coffee cakes for you. I see you had it all set up."

"I do, but you don't need to …"

Her mother raised her hand. "Go on, both of you. I'm sure you're exhausted."

Her father frowned. "What?"

He looked at Seth and then at the stairs.

"Dan, come help me," her mom said and crossed her arms, giving him the stink eye.

"But …" Her father turned toward the stairs and pointed.

"Dan. Now," her mom snapped, and Allison hid her smile behind Seth's arm.

He glared at Seth and then at his wife. "Fine."

Her parents followed Ken into the bakery, and the door shut. "Your mom is a feisty woman."

"Where do you think I got it from?" Allison asked as they walked up the stairs. They opened the door, and Gomer met them with a wagging tail.

"Hey, boy." Seth bent down. "Who put you up here?"

"Probably Mom," Allison said. "I think my dad just figured out we're serious."

"Yeah, I watched that happen," Seth said, laughing. "I'll take him out and be right back up."

Allison nodded and pulled out her phone. The text was quick and simple.

Thank you, Mom.

A winky emoji came back almost instantly.

Allison took off her hoodie and dropped it on the couch. Then she draped her shirt over the back of the chair. Her socks and shoes were left at the door, while her jeans were on the bathroom doorknob and her bra and underwear on the knob of her door. A trail straight to her bedroom. She smiled and walked into her room, then pulled back the blanket and slipped under the covers. She heard Seth come in. It took less than a minute for the door to open. He had her clothes in one hand. "I seem to have found something that belongs to you."

"Yes, yes, you have," she purred from under the covers.

"Damn." Seth's voice was two octaves lower. He stripped and crawled over her. "Allison." He said her name like it was a prayer.

And then he slid under the covers and pulled her into his arms. She didn't hesitate. Instead, she melted against him, arms around his waist, face pressed to his chest. His scent was warm, and more, he was her safety, her protector. That realization washed over her. She let the sensation sink in. He was hers. She'd found that special connection when she hadn't been looking for it. But tonight, she'd almost lost everything.

"I thought …" Her voice cracked. "I thought I'd lost you."

"You didn't," he murmured into her hair. His lips trailed to her neck. "You won't."

She tilted her face to see him. "People say that all the time. You can't know that."

"But I do know it. I knew I had the advantage over him. He was fighting out of pure rage. I was fighting for us, for our future, and for moments like these. He never stood a chance, babe."

Something inside her gave way, and she kissed him; it wasn't soft or gentle. She needed to feel him. The kiss was desperate. Her fingers gripped his arms, keeping him against her. His mouth met hers in a rush of need and heat. No hesitation and no holding back. The awkwardness of the first time was forgotten. She moved to cradle him in her legs.

"Don't go slow," she whispered.

He lifted his head, staring down at her, and she could see him in the moonlight. His eyes were dark and intense. His voice was husky when he asked, "Are you sure?"

She nodded. "I need you."

There were no words after that. Now, it was just a dance she knew. Skin touching skin, breath mingling, and sheets rustling as they spun to music only they could hear. His hands moved to her hips. Her lips on his jaw. Tangled with emotion and need, she arched beneath him, every nerve alive, every part of her wanting him.

He moved with purpose, but with a tenderness that churned her feelings into something so intense she didn't want to name it. And when release came unexpectedly, she cried out his name. Because he owned her heart and soul; he *owned* her. She'd given him full access, and he'd scooped her up like she was precious. Her heart flooded with emotion that hurt; it was so intense.

Afterward, he didn't move far. Just pulled her

closer and wrapped himself around her. She felt protected. Possessed. And she reveled in the feeling.

She lay against his chest, listening to the steady rhythm of his heartbeat. His hand repeatedly ran down the length of her hair.

"Seth?"

"Yeah, baby."

"I don't want to lose this."

He kissed her hair. "You're not going to lose me. You couldn't pry me away from you with a crowbar. I love you."

She looked up, her voice fierce. "You better, because I love you, too."

"You'll never regret it." He held her tighter. "That's my vow to you."

And in that quiet, perfect moment, she believed him.

EPILOGUE

The Christmas festival was in full swing. Allison and Seth were on the dance floor, as were most couples living around Hollister. Gregg took a sip of the soda in his hand and searched through the crush of people. The music changed, and Seth led Allison off the dance floor. He kissed her, and she went in one direction, while Seth headed his way. "How are you doing, man?" Seth asked as he extended his hand.

"Making it." Gregg nodded to where Allison disappeared. "You two good?"

"Yep. She's moved in with me and Chester. Lottie is staying in her apartment."

"Good." Gregg's eyes darted around. "She here?"

Seth chuckled. "Allison went to get her. She's still a bit shaky about being out at night alone."

"Can understand that." Gregg took another sip of his soda. "How's Chester?"

Seth sighed and shook his head. "That damn disease is taking him away from me faster than the doctor thought it would. Most days now, he just sits and looks out the window. Allison brings out Delbert every afternoon so they can whittle on the back porch. I put in heaters out there. Dad doesn't whittle anymore. Just holds the block of wood. I think Delbert knows time is slipping by. He talks to Dad about shit that happened a long time ago. Never minds that Dad doesn't respond much." Seth swallowed. "It's hard."

"What can I do to help?" Gregg would do anything he could for Seth and Allison. They were his friends, and he didn't have many.

"Nothing. Not anything anyone can do." Seth shrugged. "Mr. Marshall is working with me on my hours, but you know that. I'm set up good. The nurse is there at nine, and then I go to work. Allison is home by three. The nurse is a cool guy. Dad seems to be okay with him, so we're treading water."

"I get it. If you ever need anything, you only need to ask." He'd never had a good family dynamic. His father had put distance between him and his brother Christian. Distance he was pretty damn sure couldn't be traveled. He wished it could, but ...

"Here she is," Allison said, pulling Lottie behind her. Gregg smiled. Lottie had curled her hair, and her soft pink sweater matched the color of her cheeks.

"You look beautiful." Gregg blinked at his own words. "Ah ... I mean ..."

"Take the win, brother," Seth said and grabbed Allison. "Dance with me, woman." Allison laughed as Seth spun her onto the floor.

"Thank you," Lottie said and stepped closer to him, or farther away from the crowd. He wasn't sure which.

"Can I get you something to drink?" Gregg asked.

"No, I'm fine." Lottie shook her head.

"Heard anything about asshat?" That was what they'd been calling her ex.

"Grand Jury indicted him. Ken said he's got the evidence to make him go away for a long time."

"Did he get out on bond or bail?"

"Yeah, but he has an ankle monitor. Every time he steps out of the house, it goes off." She looked up at him. "You haven't been to town for a while. I was hoping you'd stop by the bakery."

"You were?" Gregg cleared his throat and tried that again. This time, hopefully, he wouldn't sound like a scared mouse. "You were?"

She smiled at him. "You said we could talk."

He nodded. "I meant it."

Lottie took a deep breath. "I might not be ready for anything more for a long time."

Gregg put his soda down and turned to look at her. "Lottie, nothing good runs in my blood. My father and my brother were monsters. You don't want to put your sights on me. I'm irredeemable."

She looked at him. "Allison told me about them and what happened." She bit her bottom lip. "When was the last time you hurt someone?"

"My brother. Years ago." He could remember the last punch he'd thrown. Fuck, it made him sick to think of it.

"Because your father forced you," she said, pulling him out of the memory.

"Yeah."

"I think both of us were used, Gregg. I need a friend now. Someone who knows about the night terrors and the guilt."

"God." Gregg sighed and relaxed. "The guilt rides you hard, doesn't it?"

She nodded. "Can we talk? Can we be friends?"

"We can do that." Gregg motioned to a table that had freed up. "Let's go sit down."

"I'd like that." Lottie headed toward the table, and he followed. If he weren't tainted, if his blood weren't ruined … Lottie would be the kind of woman he'd fall for …

ALSO BY KRIS MICHAELS

Guardian Security Dynasty Series

Legacy's Call

Legacy's Destiny

Throne of Secrets

Echoes of Oaths

Heir of Honor

Heir of Courage

Heir of Shadows

Veil of Secrets

Kings of the Guardian Series

Jacob: Kings of the Guardian Book 1

Joseph: Kings of the Guardian Book 2

Adam: Kings of the Guardian Book 3

Jason: Kings of the Guardian Book 4

Jared: Kings of the Guardian Book 5

Jasmine: Kings of the Guardian Book 6

Chief: The Kings of Guardian Book 7

Jewell: Kings of the Guardian Book 8

Jade: Kings of the Guardian Book 9

Justin: Kings of the Guardian Book 10

Christmas with the Kings

Drake: Kings of the Guardian Book 11

Dixon: Kings of the Guardian Book 12

Passages: The Kings of Guardian Book 13

Promises: The Kings of Guardian Book 14

The Siege: Book One, The Kings of Guardian Book 15

The Siege: Book Two, The Kings of Guardian Book 16

A Backwater Blessing: A Kings of Guardian Crossover Novella

Montana Guardian: A Kings of Guardian Novella

Guardian Defenders Series

Gabriel

Maliki

John

Jeremiah

Frank

Creed

Sage

Bear

Billy

Elliot

Guardian Security Shadow World

Anubis (Guardian Shadow World Book 1)

Asp (Guardian Shadow World Book 2)

Lycos (Guardian Shadow World Book 3)

Thanatos (Guardian Shadow World Book 4)

Tempest (Guardian Shadow World Book 5)

Smoke (Guardian Shadow World Book 6)

Reaper (Guardian Shadow World Book 7)

Phoenix (Guardian Shadow World Book 8)

Valkyrie (Guardian Shadow World Book 9)

Flack (Guardian Shadow World Book 10)

Ice (Guardian Shadow World Book 11)

Malice (Guardian Shadow World Book 12)

Harbinger (Guardian Shadow World Book 13)

Centurion (Guardian Shadow World Book 14)

Maximus (Guardian Shadow World Book 15)

Hollister (A Guardian Crossover Series)

Andrew (Hollister-Book 1)

Searching for Home (A Hollister-Guardian Crossover Novel)

Zeke (Hollister-Book 2)

Declan (Hollister- Book 3)

A Home for Love (A Hollister Crossover Novel)

Ken (Hollister - Book 4)

Finally Home (A Hollister Crossover Novel)

Barry (Hollister - Book 5)

Hope City

Hope City - Brock

HOPE CITY - Brody- Book 3

Hope City - Ryker - Book 5

Hope City - Killian - Book 8

Hope City - Blayze - Book 10

The Long Road Home

Season One:

My Heart's Home

Season Two:

Searching for Home (A Hollister-Guardian Crossover Novel)

Season Three:

A Home for Love (A Hollister Crossover Novel)

Season Four:

Finally Home (A Hollister Crossover Novel)

STAND-ALONE NOVELS

A Heart's Desire - Stand Alone

Hot SEAL, Single Malt (SEALs in Paradise)

Hot SEAL, Savannah Nights (SEALs in Paradise)

Hot SEAL, Silent Knight (SEALs in Paradise)

Join my newsletter for fun updates and release information!

>>>Kris' Newsletter<<<

ABOUT THE AUTHOR

Kris Michaels' writing career is marked by 23 appearances on the USA Today Bestseller list and three on the Wall Street Journal Bestselling list for her full-length novels. As a writer, she is known for her compelling romantic stories set against military and law enforcement backdrops, as demonstrated in her series, The Kings of Guardian, Guardian Defenders, and Guardian Security Shadow World.

Originally from South Dakota, Kris's journey from a small-town high school to a twenty-two-year career in the military set the stage for her writing career, providing a wealth of experiences and backgrounds for her characters. Now living on the Gulf Coast, she writes full-time, focusing on creating stories that merge romantic elements with suspense and action. Kris explores the themes of love, duty, and bravery, which appeal to a wide audience.

Made in United States
Cleveland, OH
29 September 2025